THE CUBS AND OTHER STORIES

The Cubs and Other Stories

The Time of the Hero

The Green House

Captain Pantoja and the Special Service

Conversation in the Cathedral

Aunt Julia and the Scriptwriter

The War of the End of the World

The Real Life of Alejandro Mayta

The Perpetual Orgy

Who Killed Palomino Molero?

The Storyteller

Mario Vargas Llosa

THE CUBS

and Other Stories

Translated from the Spanish by

Gregory Kolovakos and Ronald Christ

The Noonday Press

Farrar, Straus and Giroux

New York

English translation © 1979 by Harper and Row, Publishers, Inc.
"The Cubs" was originally published in Spanish as *Los Cachorros*,
© 1967 by Editorial Lumen Barcelona, by Industrias Gráficas
Francisco Casamajo

The remaining stories in this collection first appeared in
Spanish in *Los Jefes*, © 1965 by Mario Vargas Llosa, published
by Jorge Álvares Colección Narradores Americanos

Designed by Sidney Feinberg
Published in Canada by Collins Publishers, Toronto
Published originally in hardcover by Harper and Row, Publishers, Inc.
First edition, 1975
Noonday Press edition, 1989

Library of Congress Cataloging in Publication Data
Vargas Llosa, Mario.
   The cubs and other stories.
   Translation of Los jefes.
   CONTENTS: The cubs.—The leaders.—The grandfather.—A visitor.—On
Sunday.—The challenge.—The younger brother.
   I. Title
PZ4.V297Cu   [PQ8498.32.A65]   863   78-20217

To the memory

of Sebastián Salazar Bondy

Contents

Translators' Note

Begun as long ago as 1968, this translation would never have achieved even its present state without the continuing advice of many readers. To be sure, none of them is responsible for any errors or infelicities that may be found here; on the other hand, the translators recognize that much of whatever may be good in our work is owing to these readers, among whom we are pleased, and most grateful, to acknowledge Gene Bell-Villada, Luis Harss, José Miguel Oviedo, Colonel Fred Woerner and, of course, Mario Vargas Llosa himself.

GREGORY KOLOVAKOS
RONALD CHRIST

Author's Preface

The six short stories from *The Leaders* are a handful of survivors out of the many I wrote and tore up between 1953 and 1957, while I was still a student in Lima. I have a certain fondness for them, because they remind me of those difficult years when, even though literature mattered more to me than anything else in the world, it never entered my mind that one day I would be a writer—in the real sense of that word. I had married early and my life was smothered by jobs to earn a living as well as by classes at the university. But more than the stories I wrote on the run, what I remember from those years are the authors I discovered, the beloved books I read with the voracity that characterizes one's addiction to literature at the age of eighteen. How did I manage to read them with all the work I had? By doing only half of it or doing it very poorly. I read on buses and in classrooms, in offices and on the street, in the midst of noise and people, standing still or walking, just so long as there was a little light. My ability to concentrate was such that nothing or no one could distract me from a book. (I've lost that ability.) I remember some feats: *The Brothers Karamazov* read in one Sunday; that white night with the

French version of Henry Miller's *Tropics,* which a friend had lent me for a few hours; my astonishment at the first novels by Faulkner that fell into my hands: *The Wild Palms, As I Lay Dying, Light in August,* which I read and reread with paper and pencil as if they were textbooks.

Those readings saturate my first book. It's easy for me to recognize them in it now, but that wasn't the case when I wrote the stories. The earliest of them, "The Leaders," ostensibly re-creates a strike that we, the graduating students at the San Miguel Academy in Piura, attempted and deservedly failed at. But it's an out-of-tune echo of Malraux's novel *Man's Hope,* which I was reading while I wrote the story.

"The Challenge" is a memorable story, but for reasons the reader cannot share. A Parisian art and travel magazine —*La Revue Française*—was devoting an issue to the land of the Incas and consequently organized a contest for Peruvian stories offering a first prize of nothing less than a two-week trip to Paris with reservations at the Napoleon Hotel, from whose windows the Arch of Triumph could be seen. Naturally, there was an epidemic of literary vocation throughout Peru and hundreds of stories were entered in the competition. My heart beats fast all over again when I recall my best friend entering the booth where I was writing news for a radio broadcast to tell me that "The Challenge" had won the prize and that Paris was waiting for me with a welcoming band of musicians. The trip was literally unforgettable and full of livelier episodes than the story offered me. I wasn't able to see my idol of the moment— Sartre—but I did meet Camus, whom I approached with as much audacity as impertinence at the exit of the theater where a revival of *Les justes* was being staged; and I inflicted on him a little eight-page magazine that three of us were bringing out in Lima. (His good Spanish surprised me.) At the Napoleon I discovered that my neighbor across the hall was another laureate who was enjoying two free weeks at the hotel—Miss France of 1957—and I was terribly embarrassed at Chez Pescadou (the hotel restaurant, which I entered on tiptoe for fear of wrinkling the carpet) when they handed me a net and indicated that I should fish in the dining room tank for the trout I had chosen from the menu in complete ignorance.

I liked Faulkner but I imitated Hemingway. These stories owe a great deal to that legendary figure, who came to Peru just at that time to fish for dolphin and hunt whales. His stay left us with a shower of adventure stories, spare dialogues, clinical descriptions and bits of information withheld from the reader. Hemingway was good reading for a Peruvian who started writing a quarter of a century ago: a lesson in stylistic abstinence and objectivity. Although it had gone out of style elsewhere, we were still practicing a literature about country girls raped by despicable landowners, a literature written in purple prose that the critics used to call "telluric." I hated it for being a cheat, since its authors seemed to believe that denouncing injustice excused them from all artistic and even grammatical concerns; nevertheless, I admit that my distrust did not prevent me from lighting a candle at that altar, because "The Younger Brother" lapses into indigenist themes, flavored, perhaps, with motives originating in another of my passions of that period: Hollywood westerns.

"The Grandfather" is out of key in this suite of adolescent and *machista* stories. It, too, is a leftover from my reading—two beautiful, perverse books by Paul Bowles, *A Delicate Prey* and *The Sheltering Sky*—and of a summer in Lima filled with decadent actions: we used to go to the

Surca cemetery at midnight, we worshipped Poe and, hoping to achieve satanism someday, we consoled ourselves with spiritism. The spirits dictated all their messages to the medium, a relative of mine, with identical mistakes in spelling. Those were intense and sleepless nights, because while the séances left us skeptical about the beyond, they put our nerves on edge. Judging by "The Grandfather," I was wise not to persist in the genre of diabolism.

"On Sunday" is the story in this collection whose life I would spare. The institution of the *barrio*—a fellowship of girls and boys with their own territory, a magical space for the human game described by Huizinga—is now obsolete in Miraflores. The reason is simple: nowadays, as soon as they stop crawling, the young people of Lima have their own bicycles, motorcycles or cars that carry them great distances and bring them back to their homes. In this way, each one of them establishes a geography of friends whose routes spread across the city. But thirty years ago we had only roller skates, which hardly let us go around the block, and even those who did go by bicycle didn't get much farther since their parents forbade it. (And in those days, parents were obeyed.) So we boys and girls were condemned to our *barrio,* an extension of the home, a kingdom of friendship. Nor should *barrio* be confused with "gang" as it is known in the United States—masculine, bullyish, gangsterish. The *barrio* in Miraflores was innocent: a parallel family, a mixed tribe where you learned to smoke, dance, play sports and open your heart to girls. The concerns were not very elevated: they came down to enjoying yourself to the hilt every holiday and every summer. The great pleasures were surfing and playing soccer, dancing the mambo gracefully and switching couples after a while. I grant that we were rather silly, more uncultured than our

older brothers and sisters—which is already saying a lot—
and blind to what was going on in the immense country of
hungry people that was ours. Later on we would discover
all that, as well as what good fortune had been ours in
having lived in Miraflores and having had a *barrio!* And
retroactively, at a given moment, we came to feel ashamed.
That was silly too: one doesn't choose one's childhood. As
for me, my warmest memories are all linked to those *barrio*
rites out of which—nostalgia blended in—I wrote "On Sunday."

The *barrio* is also the theme of "The Cubs." Yet this story
is no youthful transgression but something I wrote as an
adult in Paris in 1965. I say "wrote" and I should say
"rewrote," because I made at least a dozen versions of the
story, which never worked out. It had been going through
my mind ever since I had read in a newspaper about a dog's
emasculating a newborn child in the Andes. From then on
I dreamed of a story about this strange wound that, in
contrast to others, time would open rather than close.
Simultaneously, I was turning over in my mind the idea for
a short novel about a *barrio:* its character, its myths, its
liturgy. When I decided to merge the two projects, the
problems started. Who was going to narrate the story of the
mutilated boy? The *barrio.* How to ensure that the collec-
tive narrator didn't drown out the various voices speaking
for themselves? Bit by bit, filling up my wastebasket with
torn sheets of paper, that choral voice gradually took
shape, dissolving into individual voices and coming together again in one that gives expression to the entire
group. I wanted "The Cubs" to be a story more sung than
told and, therefore, each syllable was chosen as much for
musical as for narrative reasons. I don't know why, but I felt
in this case that the verisimilitude depended on the reader's

having the impression of listening, not reading, that the story should get to him through his ears. These, shall we say, technical problems were what absorbed me. Imagine my surprise, then, at the variety of interpretations that P.P. Cuéllar's misadventures deserved: the parable of an impotent social class, castration of the artist in the underdeveloped world, a paraphrase of the aphasia among young people brought on by comic strip culture, a metaphor of my own ineptitude as a narrator. Why not? Any one of these may be correct. One thing I have learned from writing is that in this craft nothing is ever entirely clear: truth is a lie and the lie truth, and no one knows for whom it works. What's certain is that literature does not solve problems— instead, it creates them—and rather than happy, it makes people more apt to be unhappy. That's how it is and it's all part of my way of living and I wouldn't change it for any other.

Lima
February 1979

THE CUBS AND OTHER STORIES

The Cubs

1.

They were still wearing short pants that year, we weren't
smoking yet, they preferred soccer to all the other sports
and we were learning to surf, to dive from the high board
at the Terraces Club, and they were devilish, smooth-
cheeked, curious, very agile, voracious. That year, when
Cuéllar enrolled in the Champagnat Academy.

Brother Leoncio, is it true a new boy's coming? into 3A,
Brother? Yes, with his fist Brother Leoncio pushed back the
forelock hanging in his face, now let's have some quiet.

He appeared one morning at inspection time, holding his
father's hand, and Brother Leoncio put him at the head of
the line because he was even shorter than Rojas, and in
class Brother Leoncio sat him in the back with us, at that
vacant desk, young man. What's your name? Cuéllar, and
yours? Choto, and yours? Chingolo, and yours? Manny,
and yours? Lalo. From Miraflores? Yes, since last month,
before that I was living on San Antonio and now on Mariscal Castilla, near the Colina movie theater.

He was a grade grubber (but no apple polisher): the first
week he came out fifth and afterwards always first until the

accident, then he started goofing off and getting bad grades. The fourteen Incas, Cuéllar, Brother Leoncio would say, and he would recite them without taking a breath, the Ten Commandments, the three stanzas of the Marist Hymn, the poem "My Flag" by López Albujar—without taking a breath. What a whiz kid, Cuéllar, Lalo said to him and Brother a very good memory, young man, and to us, follow his example, you rascals. He would polish his nails on the lapel of his jacket and look at the whole class over his shoulder, showing off (well, not really, at heart he wasn't a show-off, just a little goofy and lots of fun. And, besides, a good pal. He'd whisper answers to us during tests and during recess he'd offer us lollipops, money bags, taffy, lucky stiff, Choto would say to him, they give you a bigger allowance than all four of us get, and he 'cause he pulled good grades and us it's not so bad 'cause you're an okay guy, you little grade grubber, that saved him).

Classes for the lower grades let out at four, at four-ten Brother Luke had them break ranks and at a quarter after four they were on the soccer field. They would throw their books on the grass, their jackets, their ties, hurry up Chingolo, hurry up, get to the goal before the others grab it, and in his cage Judas went crazy, gr-r-r, his tail stood straight up, gr-r-r gr-r-r, he bared his fangs, gr-r-r gr-r-r gr-r-r, he jumped in somersaults, gr-r-r gr-r-r gr-r-r gr-r-r, he shook the wire fence. Jeez, if he escapes one day, Chingolo said, and Manny if he escapes you gotta stay quiet, Great Danes only bit when they smelled that you're scared of them, who told you? my old man, and Choto I'd climb on top of the goal, he couldn't reach up there and Cuéllar took out his penknife and swish swish he was dreaming it, he was slicing away and burrrrryiiin, looking up at the sky, iiiiiinnnnnggg, his two hands over his mouth, ahahahhh: you like how I imitated Tarzan's yell? They only played until five o'clock, well at that hour the upper classes let out and the big guys ran us off the field like it or lump it. Tongues hanging out, brushing ourselves off and sweating they picked up their books, jackets and ties and we went out onto the street. They went down the crosstown avenue shooting baskets with their book bags, get this one, baby, we crossed the park up near Delicacies, I got it, did ya see, babe, and in the D'Onofrio candy shop on the corner we bought ice cream cones, vanilla? combo? pile on a little more, man, no gypping, a little lemon, stingy, a little extra strawberry. And then they continued along the crosstown avenue, the Gypsy's Guitar, not talking, Porta Street, absorbed in their ice cream, a traffic light, shhlp sucking shhlp and crossing over to the St. Nicholas Building and there Cuéllar said good-bye, man, don't go yet, let's go to Terraces they'd ask Chino for his ball, don't you want to try out for the class team? man, you'd have to train a little for that, c'mon, let's go, let's get a move on, just till six a quick game of soccer at Terraces, Cuéllar. He couldn't, his father wouldn't let him, he had to do his homework. They walked him home, how was he going to make the class team if he didn't practice? and we finally ended up going to Terraces alone. Nice guy but a real bookworm, Choto said, he neglects sports for his studies, and Lalo it wasn't his fault, his old man must be a ball breaker, and Chingolo sure, he was dying to come with them and Manny it was going to be real hard for him to make the team, he doesn't have the build, no kick, no stamina, he poops out right there, no nothing. Still, he butts well, Choto said, and besides he was our buddy, he had to get on somehow Lalo was saying, and Chingolo so he's with us and Manny, yeah, we'd get him on, but it was going to be tough work!

But Cuéllar, who was stubborn and dying to play on the team, practiced so much in the winter that the following year he was picked for the left inside forward position on the class team: mens sanà in corpore sano, Brother Augustine said, now did we see? you can be a good athlete and zealous in your studies, that we should follow his example. How'd you do it? Lalo asked him, where'd you get that control, those passes, that grip on the ball, those angle shots. And he: his cousin Sparky had trained him, and his father took him to the stadium every Sunday and there, watching the pros, he learned their tricks, did we catch on? He had spent the three months without going to the movies or the beach, just watching and playing soccer morning and afternoon, feel these calves, hadn't they firmed up? Yes, he's gotten a lot better, Choto was saying to Brother Luke, the coach, really, and Lalo he's a fast, hardworking forward, and Chingolo he sure organized that offense swell and, especially, he never lost his morale, and Manny did you see how he comes right down to the goal to get the ball when the opposition's got it, Brother Luke? we have to put him on the team. Cuéllar laughed happily, blew on his fingernails and polished them on his 4A jersey, white sleeves and blue chest: you're already on, we told him, we already got you on but don't let it go to your head.

In July, for the intramural championship, Brother Augustine authorized the 4A team to practice two times a week, Mondays and Fridays at the hour for drawing and music. After the second recess, when the courtyard was left empty, dampened by the drizzle, polished like a brand-new boot, the chosen eleven went down to the field, we changed uniforms and, with soccer shoes and black warm-up suits, they came out of the changing room Indian file, jogging, led by Lalo, the captain. At every schoolroom window appeared

envious faces to catch a glimpse of them running laps, there
was a cold breeze wrinkling the water of the swimming pool
(would you go swimming? after the match, not now, brrr
it's cold), of their goal kicks, and stirring the crowns of the
eucalyptus and fig trees in the park peeping over the academy's yellow wall, of their penalty kicks, and the morning
flew by: great practice, said Cuéllar, terrific, we'll win. An
hour later Brother Luke blew his whistle and, while the
classrooms were emptying out and the grades were lining
up in the courtyard, we team members got dressed to go
home for lunch. But Cuéllar lagged behind because (you
copy all the pro shots, said Chingolo, who'd ya think ya are?
Toto Terry?) he always jumped into the shower after practice. Sometimes they all showered, gr-r-r, but that day,
gr-r-r gr-r-r, when Judas appeared in the doorway to the
locker room, gr-r-r gr-r-r gr-r-r, only Lalo and Cuéllar were
washing up: gr-r-r gr-r-r gr-r-r gr-r-r. Choto, Chingolo and
Manny jumped out the windows, Lalo screamed he escaped
look man and he managed to shut the shower door right on
the Great Dane's snout. There, shrunk back, white tiles and
trickles of water, trembling, he heard Judas's barking, Cuéllar's sobbing and only barking and a lot later, I swear to you
(but how much later, asked Chingolo, two minutes? longer
man, and Choto five? longer much longer), Brother Luke's
booming voice, Brother Leoncio's curses (in Spanish,
Lalo? yeah, and in French too, did you understand him? no,
but you could tell they were curses, stupid, from the anger
in his voice), the shits, the my Gods, the get outs, the
scrams, the get losts, the get goings, the brothers' desperation, their terrible fright. He opened the door and already
they were carrying him out, wrapped up, you could hardly
see him between the black robes, passed out? yeah, naked,
Lalo? yeah, and bleeding, man, I swear, it was horrible: the

whole shower was pure blood. What else, what happened afterwards while I was getting dressed, Lalo asked, and Chingolo Brother Augustine and Brother Luke put Cuéllar in the school station wagon, we saw them from the stairway and Choto and Manny they tore off at high speed, honking and honking the horn like firemen, like an ambulance. Meanwhile, Brother Leoncio was chasing Judas who was racing back and forth in the yard, taking leaps and tumbles, he grabbed him and pushed him into his cage and between the wires (he wanted to kill him, Choto said, you should have seen him, it was scary) he whipped him savagely, beet red, his forelock bobbing in his face.

That week, Sunday mass, the Friday rosary and the prayers at the beginning and end of the classes were for Cuéllar's recovery, but the brothers got furious if the students talked among themselves about the accident, they grabbed us and a whack on the head, silence, take that, detention until six. Still, that was the only topic of conversation during recess and in classes, and the following Monday when school let out they went to visit him in the American Clinic, we saw that he didn't have a scratch on his face or hands. He was in a nice little room, hi Cuéllar, white walls and cream curtains, better already, pal? alongside a garden with little flowers, grass and a tree. They we're getting even, Cuéllar, every recess pelting Judas's cage with stone after stone, and he that's great, soon there won't be one unbroken bone in that bastard, he laughed, when he got out we'd go to the academy at night and climb in over the roof, long live the kid, pow pow, the Masked Eagle, swoosh swoosh, and we'd make him see stars, in good humor but so skinny and pale, that dog, like he did to me. Seated at the head of Cuéllar's bed were two ladies who gave us chocolates and went out into the garden, sweetie, you go on talking with your friends, they'd smoke a cigarette and come back, the one in the white dress is my mother, the other's an aunt. C'mon, tell us, Cuéllar, what happened, did he hurt you bad? real bad, where had he bitten him? well, was it right there and he got jittery, on your peepee? yes, blushing scarlet, and he laughed and we laughed and the ladies from the window hello, hello, sweetie and to us only a little longer, a secret, his old man didn't want, either did his old lady, anybody to know, my boy, better if you don't say anything, what for? it was only on the leg, sweetie, okay? The operation took two hours, he told them, he'd be back to school in ten days, look at all the vacation, how lucky you are the doctor had said to him. We left and in class everybody wanted to know, they sewed up his belly, right? with needle and thread, right? And Chingolo how embarrassed when he told us, maybe it was a sin to talk about that? Lalo no, how could it be, every night before going to bed his mother asked him did you brush your teeth? did you make weewee? and Manny poor Cuéllar, what a lot of pain he must've been in, if a ball hits you there it'd knock anybody out what would a bite be like and especially think about Judas's fangs, pick up some stones, let's get out on the field, one, two, three, gr-r-r gr-r-r gr-r-r gr-r-r, how'd you like that? bastard, take that and that'll teach you. Poor Cuéllar, Choto said, he won't be able to shine in the championship match beginning tomorrow, and Manny all that practicing for nothing and what's worse is, Lalo was saying, it's crippled the team, we've got to make an all-out effort if we don't want to stay at the bottom, guys, swear you'll make an all-out push.

2.

He only went back to the academy after the national holiday and, funny thing, instead of having learned his lesson from soccer (wasn't it on account of soccer, in a way, that Judas bit him?) he came back more of a player than ever. On the other hand, studies started mattering less to him. And that was understandable, he was no fool, he didn't have to grind away anymore: he went into exams with very low averages and the brothers passed him, bad exams and excellent, miserable homework and passed. Ever since the accident they're treating you with kid gloves, we told him, you don't know a thing about fractions and, what nerve, they gave you a ninety. In addition, they had him serving at mass, Cuéllar read the catechism, carry this year's banner in the processions, erase the blackboard, sing in the chorus, pass out the notebooks, and on first Fridays he would come into breakfast even though he had not received communion. Nobody like you, said Choto, you treat yourself to the swell life, too bad Judas didn't bite us too, and he that wasn't why: the brothers made him their pet out of fear of his old man. Idiots, what have you done to my son, I'll have this academy shut down, I'll have you sent to prison, you don't know who I am, he was going to kill that damned beast as well as the rector, calm down, calm yourself down, sir, he shook him by the collar. That's how it was, honest, said Cuéllar, his old man had told his old lady and although they talked in a whisper he, from my bed in the clinic, heard them: that was why they made him their pet, nothing else. By the collar? what a liar Lalo said, and Chingolo it's got to be true, the damned animal had disappeared for some reason. They must've sold him, we said, he must've escaped, they might have given him to somebody, and Cuéllar no, no, sure that his old man came and killed him, he always did what he promised he'd do. Because one morning the cage was empty at daybreak and a week later, in place of Judas, four white bunnies. Cuéllar, take them some lettuce, oh Brother's little helper, give them some carrots, how they coddled you, change their water and be happy.

But not only the brothers had begun to spoil him, his parents had too. Now Cuéllar came to Terraces with us every afternoon to play ball (your old man doesn't get mad anymore? no more, just the opposite, he was always asking him who won the match, my team, how many goals did you score, three? great! and he don't get upset, Mama, I tore my shirt playing, it was an accident, and she silly, what did it matter, sweetheart, the girl would sew it up and you could wear it around the house, he should give her a kiss) and later we would go to the balcony of the Excelsior or the Ricardo Palma or the Leuro movie house to see serials, movies not proper for young ladies, Cantinflas and Tin Tan pictures. Every once in a while they'd raise my allowance and they buy me whatever I want, he used to tell us, he had his parents in his back pocket, they let me do whatever I like, I've got them right here, they'd do anything for me. He was the first of the five to have ice skates, a bicycle, a motorcycle, and they Cuéllar how about your old man giving us a cup for the championship, how about his taking us to the stadium pool to see Merino and Bunny Villaran swim and how about his picking us up in his car when the matinee's over, and his old man gave it to us and took us and picked us up in his car: yes, he had him right here.

Around that time, not long after the accident, they began

to call him P.P. The nickname was coined in the classroom, was it smart aleck Gumucio who made it up? sure, who else would it have been and at first Cuéllar, Brother, he was crying, they're calling me a bad name, like a queer, who? calling you what? a nasty thing, Brother, he was embarrassed to repeat it to him, stammering and the tears were pouring out, and later during the recesses the students in the other classes P.P. what happened? and the snot was dribbling out, how ya doin', and the brother, look, he ran to Leoncio, Luke, Augustine or Professor Cañon Paredes: it was him. He complained and he also became furious, what did you say, P.P. I said, white with anger, fag, his hands and voice trembling, let's see if you dare say it again, P.P., I already dared and what happened and he shut his eyes then and, just as his dad had advised him, don't let them son, he flung himself, sock 'em in the kisser, and he challenged them, stick out your foot for him, and thud, and he punched, an undercut, a header, a kick, anywhere, in the line-up or on the field, knock him down on the ground and it's over, in the classroom, at chapel, they won't bother you anymore. But he got more annoyed and they pestered him more and once, it's getting out of hand, Brother, his father came spitting nails at the rector, they were torturing his son and he wasn't going to stand for it. Let him wear the pants, let him punish those snot-faced kids or he'd do it himself, he'd put everybody in their place, what insolence, pounding the table, it was the last straw, it was the limit. But they had stuck the nickname to him like a postage stamp and, despite the brothers' punishments, despite the rector's be more humane, the rector's take a little pity on him, and despite Cuéllar's sobbing and kicking and threats and punches, the nickname got out onto the street and little by little it was making its way around the sections of Miraflores and he could never get it off his back, poor guy. P.P. pass the ball, don't be greedy, how'd you do in algebra, P.P.? P.P., I'll swap a Life Saver for a gumdrop, make sure you come tomorrow on the trip to Chosica, P.P., they'd go swimming in the river, the brothers would bring gloves and you'll be able to box with Gumucio and get back at him, P.P., got boots? because we'd have to climb the hill, P.P., and when we get back we still might make the early show, P.P., like the plan?

They too, Cuéllar, we who were careful at first, started letting it slip out, old man, against our will, brother, pal, all of a sudden P.P. and he, blushing, what? or pale, you too, Chingolo? opening his eyes wide, man, sorry, it wasn't with bad intentions, him too, his friend too? man, Cuéllar, don't be that way, if everybody called you that it was catching, you too, Choto? and it rolled off his tongue without his wanting to, he too, Manny? so that's what we were calling him behind his back? the minute he turned his back and they P.P., right? No, what an idea, we bear-hugged him, promise never again and anyway why are you getting mad, brother, it was a nickname like any other and finally don't you call lame Pérez Gimpy and cross-eyed Rodríguez Pock Face or Evil Eye and the deaf-mute Rivera Golden Tongue? And didn't they call him Choto and him Chingolo and him Manny and him Lalo? Don't get mad, brother, keep on playing, c'mon, it's your turn.

Bit by bit he was growing resigned to his nickname and by the sixth grade he did not cry or get tough anymore, he pretended not to notice and sometimes he even joked, not P.P., Big P.P. ha ha! and in the first year of junior high school he had become so accustomed to it that, instead, when they called him Cuéllar, he became serious and looked distrustfully, as if uncertain, was it a joke? He even put out his hand to new friends saying how do you do, P.P. Cuéllar, glad to meet you.

Not to girls, of course, just to men. Because at that time, besides sports, they were already interested in girls. We had started making jokes, in class, hey, yesterday I saw Martínez with his girl, during recess, they were walking hand in hand on the embankment and all of a sudden, pow, a hit! and at the end of periods, on the mouth? yes and they'd stayed a hell of a long time kissing. Soon, that was the main thing they talked about. Kiki Rojas had a girl- friend, older than him, blond, with blue eyes and on Sun- day Manny saw them going into the afternoon show at the Ricardo Palma together and after the show let out her hair was all messed up, sure they'd made out, and the next day at night Choto caught the Venezuelan in the fifth year, the one they call Jaws 'cause of his big mouth, man, in a car, with a really painted-up doll and, sure enough, they were making out, and you, Lalo, made out yet? and you, P.P., ha ha, and Manny liked Chickie Saenz's sister, and Choto was starting to pay for an ice cream and he dropped his wallet and he had a photo of some Little Red Riding Hood at a kids' party, ha ha, don't make faces, Lalo, we already know you're dying over that skinny Rojas, and you, P.P., dying for anybody? and he no, blushing, not yet, or pale, he wasn't dying over anybody, and you and you, ha ha.

If we got out at five on the button and raced down Pardo Avenue as if the devil were on our heels, we made it just as the girls were coming out of school. We would stand on the corner and look at that, there were the buses, they were the ones in third year and the one in the second window is Canepa's sister, hello, hello, and that one, look, shout hello to her, she laughed and laughed, and the girl answered us, hello, hello, but it wasn't for you, snot-nose, and that one and that one. Sometimes we brought little notes we skimmed through the air at them, you're really good-looking, I like your braids, your uniform fits you better than anybody else's, your friend Lalo, watch out, man, the nun already saw you, she's going to punish them, what's your name, I'm Manny, want to go to the movies Sunday? she should answer him tomorrow with the same kind of note or let me know shaking her head yes as the bus went by. And you Cuéllar, didn't he like any of them? yes, that one in the back, four-eyes? no, the one right next to her, then why didn't he write her? and he what would I say to her, let's see, want to be my girl? no, how dumb, he wanted to be her boyfriend and sent her a kiss, yes, that was better, but it was short, something sneakier, I want to be your friend and he was sending you a kiss and I adore you, she'd be the cow and I'll be the bull, ha ha. And now sign your first name and your last name and do a little drawing for her, what for instance? anything, a little bull, a little flower, a little peepee, and so we spent our afternoons, running after the buses of the Academy of the Indemnity and, sometimes, we went as far as Arequipa Avenue to watch the girls from Villa Maria in their white uniforms, just made your first communion? we'd shout at them, and we even took the express and got off at St. Isidor to take a look at the girls from St. Ursula and from Sacred Heart. We didn't play as much soccer as before.

When birthdays turned into mixed parties, the boys stayed out in the garden, pretending to play tag, you're it! who's got the button or ring-a-lievo, caught you! while we were all eyes, all ears, what was going on in the living room? what were the girls doing with those big guys, what envy, who already knew how to dance? Until one day they decided to learn too and then we spent Saturdays, whole

Sundays, men dancing with each other, at Lalo's house, no, at mine it's bigger, it was better, but Choto had more records, and Manny but I've got my sister who can teach us and Cuéllar, no, at his house, his parents already knew and one day, here, his mother, sweetheart, they gave him that hi-fi, just for him? sure, didn't he want to learn to dance? He'd put it in his room and call his friends and would lock himself up with them as long as he wanted and also buy records, sweetheart, go to the Record Center, and they went and we picked out huarachas, mambos, boleros and waltzes and they sent the bill to his old man, that's all, Mr. Cuéllar, 285 Mariscal Castilla. The waltz and bolero were easy, you had to remember and count, one here, one there, the music didn't matter too much. The hard ones were the huaracha, we have to learn the steps, said Cuéllar, the mambo, and to twirl and move apart and show off. We learned to dance and smoke almost at the same time, tripping over ourselves, choking on the smoke from Luckies and Viceroys, prancing until suddenly, now brother, you got it, it was coming out, don't lose it, move a little more, getting sick at our stomachs, coughing and spitting, hey did he let it out? liar, he was holding the smoke under his tongue, and P.P. me, we should count for him, did we see? eight, nine, ten and how he blew it out, did he or didn't he know how to take a drag? And also to blow it out through his nose and to squat down and twirl around and get up without losing the beat.

Before, what we liked most in the world were sports and the movies, and they would give anything for a soccer match, and now instead it was girls and dancing most and what we would give anything for was a party with Pérez Prado records and permission to smoke from the lady of the house. They had parties almost every Saturday and

when we didn't go as guests we crashed and, before entering, they would go into the corner bar and banging on the
bar with a fist, we would ask the bartender for five shots!
Bottoms up, P.P. said, like this, glub glub, like men, like me.
    When Pérez Prado came to Lima with his orchestra, we
went to wait for him at the airport, and Cuéllar, let's see,
who shoved through like me, managed to make his way
through the crowd, got up to him, grabbed him by the coat
and shouted to him: "The Mambo King!" Pérez Prado
smiled at him and also shook my hand, I swear to you, and
he signed his autograph album, look. They followed him,
lost in the caravan of fans, in Bobby Lozano's car, to Plaza
San Martin and, despite the archbishop's prohibition and
the warnings of the brothers from the Champagnat Academy, we went to the bullfight, to Sol Stadium, to see the
national mambo championship. Every night, at Cuéllar's
we'd put on El Sol Radio and listen in a frenzy, what a
trumpet, man, what a beat, the Pérez Prado broadcast, what
a piano.
    They were already wearing long pants by then, we slicked
our hair with tonic and they had grown, especially Cuéllar,
who from being the smallest and the puniest of us five
turned into the tallest and strongest. You've gotten to be
a Tarzan, P.P., we told him, what a build you're growing
muscles every day.

3.

    The first to have a girlfriend was Lalo, when we were in
our freshman year. One night he came into the Tasty
Cream, real dreamy, they what's up with you and he, beam-
ing, puffed up like a peacock: I've asked Chabuca Molina to
go steady, she said yes to me. We went to celebrate at the

Indian Messenger and with the second glass of beer, Lalo,
how did you put it to her, Cuéllar started getting a little
nervous, had he held her hand? a little annoying, what had
Chabuca done, Lalo, and full of questions, c'mon, did you
kiss her? Pleased, he told us, and now it was their turn,
cheers, butter wouldn't melt in his mouth, let's see if we'll
hurry up and get a girlfriend and Cuéllar, banging the table
with his glass, what did she say, what did you say to her,
what did you do. You sound like some priest, P.P., Lalo
said, you're giving me confession and Cuéllar, tell us, tell
us, what else. They had three beers and, at midnight, P.P.
got sick. Leaning against a lamppost, right on Larco Avenue, in front of the public clinic, he vomited: chicken, we
said to him, and also what a waste, throwing away that beer
after what it cost, what squandering. But he, you double-
crossed us, he wasn't in the mood for joking, double-
crosser Lalo, spitting up, you went ahead, puking all over
his shirt, falling for a girl, his trousers, and not even telling
us he was chasing her, P.P., bend over a little, you're making a mess of yourself, but he nothing, that just wasn't
done, what's it to you if I make a mess of myself, you lousy
friend, double-crosser. Later, while we were cleaning him
up, he cooled down, and got sentimental: we'd never see
you anymore, Lalo. He would spend Sundays with Chabuca
and you won't look for us anymore, you fairy. And Lalo
what an idea, man, my girlfriend and my friends were two
different things but they don't compete with each other,
there's no reason to be jealous, P.P., calm down, and they
shake hands but Cuéllar didn't want to, Chabuca should
shake his hand, I'm not going to shake it. We went with him
to his house and all along the way he was muttering shut
up man and swearing, we're there already, go in real slow,
real slow, tiptoe like a thief, careful, if you make a racket

your parents will wake up and catch you. But he began to shout, let's have a look, to kick his front door, let them wake up and catch him and what was going to happen, chicken, we shouldn't go, he wasn't scared of his parents, we should stay and we'd see. Something's gotten into him, said Manny, as we raced toward the crosstown street, you said I asked Chabuca to go steady and friend his face and mood changed, and Choto he was jealous, that's why he got drunk and Chingolo his parents are going to wring his neck. But they didn't do anything to him. Who opened the door for you? my mother and what happened? we asked him, she hit you? No, she started crying, sweetheart, how could you, how could he drink at his age, and my old man came in too and he bawled him out, nothing else, you'll never do this again? no Papa, wasn't he ashamed of what he'd done? yes. They gave him a bath, they put him to bed and the next morning he told them he was sorry. And Lalo too, man, I'm sorry, the beer went right to my head, see? I insulted you, I was bugging you, wasn't I? No, what garbage, a question of a few drinks, give me five and friends, P.P., like before, nothing's happened.

But something had happened: Cuéllar began to do nutty things to get attention. They gave in to him and we went along with him, how about I steal my old man's car and we drag-race along the ocean drive, guys, why not man, and he took out his dad's Chevrolet and they went to the ocean drive; how about me breaking Bobby Lozano's record? why not man, and he whoosh along the embankment from Benavides to Quebrada whoosh in two minutes fifty, did I break it, yes and Manny crossed himself, you broke it, and you, you pansy, how scared you were; how about my treating us at Tastes So Good and we play possum when the bill comes? why not man, and they went to the Tastes So Good,

we stuffed ourselves with hamburgers and milk shakes, they
left one by one and from St. Mary's Church we saw Cuéllar
dodge the waiter and get out what'd I tell you? how about
my blowing out all the windows of the house with my father's shotgun? why not P.P. and he blew them out. He
played the nut in order to get attention, but also in order
to did you see, did you see? to make fun of Lalo, you
wouldn't dare and me sure I dared. He won't forgive him
for Chabuca, we said, how he hates him.

During sophomore year, Choto asked Fina Sales to go
steady and she told him yes and Manny asked Kitty Lanas
and she too. Cuéllar locked himself up in his house for a
month and at school he hardly said hello to them, listen,
what's wrong, nothing, why don't you come looking for us,
why didn't you go out with them? he didn't feel like going
out. He's playing mysterious, they said, intriguing, kinky,
bitter. But little by little he accepted it and returned to the
group. Sundays, Chingolo and he would go to the matinee
by themselves (little bachelors, we called them, widowers),
and afterwards they would kill time any old way, hanging
around, not talking or just barely let's go here, there, hands
in their pockets, listening to records at Cuéllar's, reading
comics or playing cards, and at nine they'd drop down to
Salazar Park to look for the others, because at that hour we
were already saying good night to our girlfriends. Did you
make out asked Cuéllar, as we took off our coats, loosened
our ties and rolled up our sleeves at the pool hall on
Ricardo Palma Avenue, really made out, guys? his voice
sick with annoyance, jealousy and irritation, and they shut
up, let's play, hand, tongue? blinking as if the smoke and
the light from the bulbs were hurting his eyes, and we it
made him mad, P.P.? instead of getting annoyed, why don't
you get yourself a chick and stop being a pain in the ass?

and he did they French-kiss you, hacking and spitting like
a drunk, till they gagged? tapping his heels, did you lift
their skirts, get your pinkie in? and they the envy was eating
away at him, P.P., really taste good, really nice? it was
driving him crazy, better if he shut up and got started. But,
never wearing down, he kept at it, now, for real, what had
we done with them? how long did the girls let you kiss
them? still at it, buddy? shut up, he was being a pain now,
and one time Lalo got mad: shit, he was going to smash his
face in, he was making like our girlfriends were putting out.
We separated them and got them to be friends again, but
Cuéllar couldn't, it was stronger than he was, every Sunday
the same crap: come on, how did it go? we should tell him
everything, good making out?

In our senior year, Chingolo asked Baby Romero to go
steady and she told him no, Tula Ramírez and she no,
China Saldivar and she yes, third try's the winner, he said,
if at first you don't succeed try, try again, happy. We cele-
brated in the wrestlers' bar on San Martin Street. Silent,
sulky, hunched over in his corner chair, Cuéllar downed
shot after shot, stop pulling that long face, man, now it was
his turn. He should pick out some chick and she'd fall for
him, we told him, we'll do the spadework for you, we would
help him and our girlfriends would too. Sure, sure, I'll pick
soon, shot after shot, and suddenly, bye, he stood up: he
was tired, I'm going home to bed. If he stayed he was going
to cry, Manny said, and Choto because he was bottling up
the urge, and Chingolo if he didn't cry he was going to
throw a fit like that other time. And Lalo: they ought to help
him out, he was talking serious, we'd get him a chick even
if she was a dog, and his complex would disappear. Sure,
sure, we would help him, he was a good guy, a little touchy
sometimes but anybody in his situation, it was understand-

able, he was forgiven, he was missed, he was liked, let's drink to him, P.P., clink glasses, here's to you.

After that, Cuéllar went to Sunday and holiday matinees all alone—we would see him in the back of the orchestra, slouched in the back rows, lighting up butt after butt, sneaking looks at the couples making out—and he got together with them only at night, at the pool hall, at Bransa, at the Tasty Cream, his face sour, good Sunday? and his voice sharp, he fine and you guys really great I bet, right?

But by summer his snit was over. We went to the beach together—to Horseshoe, not to Miraflores anymore—in the car his parents had given him for Christmas, a Ford convertible with no muffler, it paid no attention to traffic signals and deafened, terrified the pedestrians. For better or worse, he had made friends with the girls and got along with them all right, in spite of always, Cuéllar, they went around pestering him with the same thing: why don't you ask some girl to go steady right now? So they would be five couples and we would go out in a pack all the time and they would be all over together, why don't you do it? Cuéllar defended himself by joking, no because then they wouldn't all fit in his mighty Ford and one of you will have to be the sacrificial victim, throwing off the scent, aren't nine too tight? Seriously, Kitty said, everybody had a girl and he no, aren't you tired of playing solo? He should chase Skinny Gamino, she's dying for you, she had admitted to them the other day, at China's house, playing truth and consequences, don't you like her? Grab her, we'd help him, she would take him, settle on it. But he did not want to have a girlfriend and he put on the face of a renegade, I like my freedom, and of a skirt chaser, he was better off single. Your freedom for what, said China, to do nasty things? and Chabuca, to go around making out? and Kitty, with cheap

girls? and he the face of a mystery man, maybe, of a pimp?
maybe and of a profligate: could be. Why don't you ever
come to our parties? said Fina, you used to come to all of
them and you were so much fun and danced so good, what
happened to you Cuéllar? And he shouldn't be such a drag,
come and sometime you'll meet a chick you like and you'll
fall for her. But he no way, waste of time, our parties bored
him, old before his time, he didn't go because he had better
ones where I enjoy myself more. What's wrong with you is
you don't like decent girls, they said, and he as friends sure
and they only the easy ones, the trashy ones, the brassy
ones and, suddenly, P.P., yes, I like I l-l-l-like, began, d-d-d-
decent g-g-girls, to stutter, j-j-j-just n-not S-s-s-ski-n-n-n-n-
ny Gamino, they you already squirmed out and he b-b-b-
besides th-th-th-there's n-no t-t-t-time f-f-for t-t-tests, and
the guys leave him alone, we stuck up for him, you're not
going to convince him, he's got his little plans, his little
secrets, step on it man, look at that sun, the Horseshoe
must be sizzling, floor the gas, make the mighty Ford fly.

We would swim in front of the Seagulls and, while the
four couples sunned themselves on the beach, Cuéllar
showed off surfing. Let's go, that one that's building,
Chabuca said, that gigantic one, can you? P.P. jumped to
his feet, she'd hit on just what he liked, at least he could
beat us at that: he was going to try it, Chabuquita, look. He
dashed—he ran sticking his chest out, throwing his head
back—he plunged into the water, pushed forward with
good strokes, kicking in unison, how good he swims said
Kitty, he reached the peak of the wave just as it was going
to break, look he's going to ride it, he dared to said China,
he stayed afloat and scarcely putting his head under, one
arm rigid and the other striking out, cutting the water like
a champion, we saw him rise to the crest of the wave, fall

with it, disappear in an uproar of foam, look, look he's going to get knocked down in one of those said Fina, and they saw him reappear and come in swept along by the wave, his body arched, his head out, his feet crossed in the air, and we saw him reach the shore effortlessly, nudged by the surf.

What a good surfer, the girls said while Cuéllar turned around against the undertow, waved good-bye to us and struck out to sea again, he was so nice, and really good-looking too, why didn't he have a girlfriend? The boys looked at each other out of the corners of their eyes, Lalo laughed, Fina what's wrong with them, why the horse laughs, tell us, Choto blushed, because that's why, it's nothing and besides what're you talking about, what horse laughs, she don't play dumb and he no, he wasn't playing dumb, honest. He didn't have one because he's shy, Chingolo said, and Kitty he wasn't, what was he going to be, more like a smart aleck and Chabuca then why not? He's hunting but not finding, said Lalo, he'll ask somebody soon and China wrong, he wasn't hunting, he never went to parties, and Chabuca then why? They know, said Lalo, cross my heart, hope to die, they know and they were playing dumb, why? in order to worm it out of them, if they didn't know how come so many whys, so many funny looks, so much bitchiness in their voices. And Choto: no, you're wrong, they didn't know, they were innocent questions, the girls felt sorry for him because he didn't have a chick at his age, they feel sorry he goes around alone, they wanted to help him. Maybe they don't know but one of these days they're going to, Chingolo said, and it'd be his fault, what would it cost him to make a pass at some girl even though it was just to throw them off the track? and Chabuca then why? and Manny what does it matter to you, don't bug him

so much, the day you least expect it he'll fall in love, she'd
see, and now keep quiet here he is.

As the days passed, Cuéllar became more stand-offish
with the girls, more tight-lipped and distant. Crazier too: he
ruined Kitty's birthday party throwing a string of firecrack-
ers through the window, she burst into tears and Manny got
mad, went to find him, they slugged each other, P.P. nailed
him. It took us a week to get them to be friends again, sorry
Manny, hell, I don't know what got into me, buddy, don't
worry, I should be asking your pardon, P.P., for getting hot
under the collar, c'mon c'mon, and Kitty forgave you too
and wants to see you; he came drunk to mass on Christmas
Eve and Lalo and Choto had to carry him dead weight out
into the park, lemme go, raving, he didn't give a damn,
puking, I wish I had a pistol, what for, buddy? with pink
elephants, to kill us? yeah and the same goes for that guy
going by pow pow and for you and for me too pow pow;
one Sunday he invaded the grounds of the Hippodrome
and with his Ford vrroom charged the crowd vrroom who
screamed and jumped the fences, terrified, vrroom. During Mardi Gras girls kept away from him: he'd bombard
them with stink bombs, eggshells, rotten fruit, balloons
filled with piss and he'd daub them with mud, ink, flour,
soap (for washing pots) and shoe polish: brute, they'd call
him, pig, beast, animal, and he'd show up at the parties at
the Terraces Club, at the kids' parties in Barranco Park, at
the Lawn Tennis Dance, without a costume, a container
of ether in each hand, eeny meeny miney mo, got her, I
got her in the eyes, ha ha, hip hip hooray, I blinded her,
ha ha, or armed with a cane to stick between the couples'
feet and make them fall down: thud. They fought, they
punched him, sometimes we'd take his side but he doesn't
learn his lesson from anything, we said, they're going to

kill him on account of something like that.

His crazy pranks earned him a bad reputation and Chingolo, brother, you've got to change, Choto, P.P., you're getting nasty, Manny, girls didn't want to get together with him anymore, they thought he was a bad egg, a swellhead, a drag. He, sometimes so sad, it was the last time, he'd change, word of honor, and sometimes such a bully, a bad egg, huh? that's what the loudmouths say about me? it didn't bother him, he'd get over the dolls, they could go shove it, up to here.

At the graduation dance—a formal, two orchestras, at the country club—the only class member not there was Cuéllar. Don't be stupid, we told him, you've got to come, we'll find a girl for you, Kitty already spoke to Margot, Fina to Ilse, China to Elena, Chabuca to Flora, they all wanted to, they're dying to be your date, take your pick and come to the dance. But he no, how dumb wearing a tux, he wouldn't go, instead let's meet later. Okay, P.P., whatever you want, don't go, you're bucking the crowd, he should wait for us at the Indian Messenger around two, we'd drop the girls off at their houses, pick him up and we'd go for a few drinks, roam around town and he getting a little sad sure.

4.

The following year, when Chingolo and Manny were in their first term of engineering, Lalo in pre-med and Choto began to work at the Wiese store and Chabuca was no longer in love with Lalo but with Chingolo and China no longer with Chingolo but with Lalo, Teresita Arrarte came to Miraflores: Cuéllar saw her and, for a little while at least, he changed. Overnight he stopped doing crazy things and walking around in shirtsleeves, dirty pants and messed-up hair. He started to wear a jacket and tie, to comb his hair in a D.A. like Elvis Presley and to shine his shoes: what's going on with you, P.P., you hardly look like yourself, cool down kid. And he, nothing, in good spirits, nothing's going on with me, you've got to keep up your appearance a little, right? blowing on, polishing his fingernails, he seemed like old times. What a surprise, boy, we told him, what a switch seeing you like this, isn't it because? and he, like a gumdrop, maybe, Terry? suddenly then, did he like her? could be, like a Chiclet, could be.

He became sociable again, almost as much as when he was a kid. Sundays he'd show up at noon mass (sometimes we saw him take communion) and when church let out he'd go up to the neighborhood girls how're you doing? What's new, Terry, were we going to the park? why didn't we sit on that bench where there was some shade. Afternoons, at dusk, he'd go down to the skating rink and he'd fall down and get up, fooling around and chattering, c'mon c'mon Teresita, he'd teach her, and if she fell? No you won't, he'd hold her hand, c'mon c'mon, around just once more, and she okay, blushing and flirting, once more but very slow, blondish, cute-assed and with her mouse teeth, let's go then. He also started hanging around the Regattas, Papa, he should become a member, all his friends went there and his old man okay, I'll buy a membership card, was he going to be a rower, son? yes, and Bowling on the crosstown street. He even took walks Sunday afternoons in Salazar Park, he always looked cheerful, Terry, know how an elephant's like Jesus, considerate, hold my glasses, Terry, the sun's very strong, talkative, what's new, Terry, everybody okay at home? and generous, a hot dog, Terry, a sandwich, a milk shake?

It's happened, said Fina, his turn came, he fell in love.

And Chabuca he was really hooked, he just looked at Terry and started drooling, and they at night around the pool table, while we waited for him will he ask her? Choto will he have the nerve? and Chingolo will Terry find out? But nobody asked him to his face and he didn't let on he understood their hints, did you see Terry? yes, did they go to the movies? to the Ava Gardner film, to the matinee, and how was it? good, terrific, we should go, they shouldn't miss it. He took off his jacket, rolled up his sleeves, grabbed the cue stick, ordered beer for five, they played and one night, after a royal carom, in a half voice, without looking at us, it's all set, they were going to cure him. He tallied his score, they were going to operate on him, and they what're you saying, P.P.? they're really going to operate on you? and he like somebody who couldn't care less pretty good, huh? It could be done, sure, not here but in New York, his old man was going to take him, and we that's great, pal, that's fantastic, that's really some piece of news, when was he going to go? and he soon, in about a month, to New York, and they he should be laughing, sing, yell, get happy, pal, hooray. Only he wasn't sure yet, he had to wait for the doctor's reply, my old man already wrote to him, not a doctor but a scientist, a real brain like they have up there and he, Papa, did it come, no, and the next day, was there any mail, Mama, no sweetheart, calm down, it'll come, no reason to get impatient and at last it came and his old man took him by the shoulder: no, it couldn't be done, son, he had to be brave. Man, what a shame, they told him, and he maybe it can someplace else, in Germany for instance, in Paris, in London, his old man was going to check, to write thousands of letters, he'd spend more than he had, boy, and he'd travel, they'd operate on him and he'd be cured, and we sure, pal, right, and when he left, poor guy, they felt like bawling.

Choto: what a rotten time Terry picked to move here, and
Chingolo he'd resigned himself and now he's desperate
and Manny but maybe later on, science was making such
progress, wasn't it? they'd discover something and Lalo no,
his uncle the doctor had told him no, there's no way, there's
no cure and Cuéllar anything Papa? not yet, from Paris,
Mama? and if suddenly in Rome? anything from Germany
yet?

And meanwhile he began going to parties again and, as
if to erase the bad reputation he had earned with his rock
'n' roll antics and to win over the parents, he behaved
himself like a model guest at birthdays and barbecues: he
came on time and without any drinks in him, a little gift in
his hand, Chabuquita, for you, happy birthday, and these
flowers for your mom, listen, did Terry get here? He
danced very stiffly, very properly, you look like an old man,
he didn't mash his partner, c'mon cutie let's dance to the
wallflowers, and he talked with the mothers, the fathers,
and he looked after may I help you ma'am the aunts, can
I pass you a little fruit juice? the uncles a drink? gallant,
how beautiful your necklace is, how your ring shines, talkative, did you go the races, sir, when is your horse coming
in first? and flattering, you're the life of the party, ma'am,
you should teach him to dip like that, Joaquin, what he'd
give to dance like that.

When we were talking, sitting on a bench in the park, and
Terry Arrarte came close, at a table in the Tasty Cream,
Cuéllar would change, or in the neighborhood the conversation: he wants to wow her, they said, pass himself off as
a brain, he milks her for admiration. He talked about
strange and difficult things: religion (being immortal, could
God, who was all-powerful, kill Himself? let's see, which one
of us solved the puzzle), politics (Hitler wasn't as crazy as

they said, in just a few short years he turned Germany into a country that bullied everybody, didn't he? what did they think), spiritism (it wasn't a matter of superstition but science, in France they had mediums at the university and they didn't only summon up spirits, they also took pictures of them, he'd seen a book, Terry, if she wanted he'd get it and I'll loan it to you). He announced that he was going to study: next year he'd enter Catholic U. and she leading him on that's good, what career was he going to pursue? and put her small white hands over his eyes, he'd pursue law, her plump fingers and long nails, law? ugh, what a bore! painted with clear polish, growing sad, and he but not to become some shyster lawyer but to enter the Ministry of Foreign Affairs and become a diplomat, growing happy, little hands, eyes, eyelashes and he yes, the minister was a friend of his old man, he'd already talked to him, a diplomat? tiny mouth, oh, how nice! and he, burning up, dying, of course, you got around a lot, and she that too and besides you spent your life at parties: blinking tiny eyes.

Love works miracles, said Kitty, how serious he's gotten, what a regular gentleman. And China: but it was the strangest sort of love, if he was so taken with Terry why didn't he ask her to go steady once and for all? and Chabuca exactly, what was he waiting for? he's been chasing her for more than two months now and till now a lot of talk and no action, what kind of a love affair's that? The guys, among themselves, do they know or are they playing dumb? but in front of the girls we stood up for him by covering up: slow and steady wins the race, girls. It's a matter of pride, said Chingolo, he doesn't want to take any chances till he's sure she'll say yes. But of course she was going to say yes, said Fina, didn't she make eyes at him, look at Lalo and China so sweet on each other, and she dropped hints for him, what a good skater you are, how gorgeous your sweater is, how warm and she even declared herself to him playing, will you be my partner? That's just why he's suspicious, said Manny, with flirts like Terry you never knew, it seemed okay and then no. But Fina and Kitty no, not true, they'd asked her will you say yes to him? and she let them understand she would, and Chabuca didn't she go out a lot with him, at parties didn't she dance only with him, at the movies did she sit with anybody else? It's clear as crystal: she's crazy for him. And China really so much waiting for him to ask was going to wear her out, tell him right away and if he wanted an opportunity we'd arrange it for him, a little party for example on Saturday, they'd dance a little while, at my house or Chabuca's or at Fina's, we'd go out into the garden and they would leave the two alone, what more could he ask. And at the pool hall: they didn't know, what babies, or what hypocrites, sure they know and they were playing dumb.

Things can't go on like this, Lalo said one day, she had him on a leash, P.P. was going to go crazy, he might even die of love, let's do something, they sure, but what, and Manny find out if Terry's really nuts over him or it's just flirting. They went to her house, we asked her, but she was the smartest girl in the world, she runs rings around the four of us, they said. Cuéllar? sitting out on the balcony of her house, but you don't call him Cuéllar but some nasty swear word, rocking herself so the light from the streetlamp would hit her legs, he's dying for me? they weren't bad, how did we know? And Choto don't play dumb, she knew it and they did too and the girls and all Miraflores talked about it and she, all eyes, mouth, little nose, really? as if she were looking at a Martian: that's the first I've heard about it. And Manny go on Terry, talk straight, out with it, didn't she realize how he looked at her? And she oh, oh, oh, clapping, little hands, teeth, tiny shoes, we should look, a butterfly! we should run, catch it and bring it to her. He'd look at her, sure, but like a friend and, besides, how pretty, stroking its little wings, little fingers, nails, tiny voice, they killed it, poor thing, he never said anything to her. And they what a story, what a lie, he must've told you something, at least he'd have flirted with her and she no, honest, she'd dig a little hole in her garden and bury it, a little lock of hair, her neck, her little ears, never, she swore to us. And Chingolo didn't she even realize how he was chasing after her? and Terry he might follow her around as a friend, oh, oh, oh, tapping her shoes together, little fists, big doll eyes, it wasn't dead, the faker, it flew away, waist and small tits, well, if not, he'd at least held her hand, hadn't he, or tried to anyway, right? there you are, right there, we should run, or he had expressed his love, right? and again we should catch it, it's that he's shy, said Lalo, hold it but be careful, you're going to smudge, and he doesn't know whether you'll say yes, Terry, was she going to say yes? and she ahh, ahh, little wrinkles, little forehead, they killed it and mangled it, little dimples on her cheeks, little eyelashes, eyebrows, who? and we what do you mean who and she better get rid of it, the way it was, all mangled, why bother burying it: a little shrug. Cuéllar? and Manny yes, she went for him? she still didn't know and Choto then you do like him, Terry, you really went for him, and she I didn't say that, only that she didn't know, she'd see if the occasion presented itself but it was sure not to and they sure it would. And Lalo did she think he was good-looking? and she Cuéllar? elbows, knees, yes, he was sort of good-looking, wasn't he? and we see, see how she liked him? and she I hadn't said that, no, we shouldn't trick her, look, the little butterfly sparkled

among the geraniums in the garden or was it some other
bug? the tip of her little toe, her foot, a tiny white heel. But
why did he have that ugly nickname, we were very ill-man-
nered, why didn't we call him something nice like we called
Chicken, Bobby, Superman or Bunny Villaran and we she
did like him, she did like him, did you see? she felt sorry
for him on account of his nickname, so she did love him,
Terry, and she loved? a little, eyes, a little burst of laughter,
just as a friend, sure.

She pretends she doesn't, we said, but there's no doubt
she does: P.P. should ask her and that'll be that, let's talk
to him. But it was hard and they didn't dare.

And as for Cuéllar, he didn't make up his mind either:
night and day he followed Terry Arrarte around, looking at
her, doing favors for her, pampering her and in Miraflores
those who didn't know made fun of him, bed warmer they
called him, what an act, skirt chaser and the girls sang to
him "how much longer, how much longer" to embarrass
and egg him on. Then, one night we took him to the Barranco movie house and, as we were leaving, man, let's go
to the Horseshoe in your mighty Ford and he okay, they'd
have a few beers and play pinball, fine. We went in his
mighty Ford, roaring, screeching around corners and at the
Chorrillos breakwater a cop stopped them, we were going
over eighty? sir, officer, don't be that way, no reason to be
tough, and he asked us for our driver's license and they had
to give him a couple of bucks, sir? have a few whiskeys on
us, officer, there's no reason to be tough, and at Horseshoe
beach they got out and sat down at a table in the National:
what a dog show, man, but that half-breed wasn't bad and
how they danced, it was better than the circus. We had a
couple of beers and they still didn't dare, four and still
nothing, six and Lalo started in. I'm your friend, P.P.,

and he laughed drunk already? and Manny we really like you a lot, man, and he yeah? laughing, an affection binge for you too? and Chingolo they wanted to talk to him, man, and also give him some advice. Cuéllar changed, grew pale, offered a toast, nice couple over there, huh? him a little runt and she a monkey, right? and Lalo why hide it, pal, you're dying for Terry aren't you? and he coughed, sneezed and Manny, P.P., level with us, yes or no? and he laughed, so sad and trembling, he almost couldn't be heard: h-h-he was d-d-d-ying, y-y-yes. Two more beers and Cuéllar didn't know wh-wh-what he was going to do, Choto, what could he do? and he ask her and he it's out of the question, Chingolito, how am I going to ask and he by asking her, pal, telling her you love her, then, she's going to say yes to you. And he it wasn't on account of that, Manny, she could say yes to him but, what about afterwards? He drank his beer and he was losing his voice and Lalo afterwards will be afterwards, ask her now and that'll be that, maybe he would be cured after a while and he, Chotito, and if Terry knew, if somebody had told her? and they she didn't know, we already made her admit, she's dying for you and he got his voice back, she's dying for me? and we yeah, and he sure maybe sometime I can get cured, did we think so? and they yeah, yeah, P.P., and anyway you can't go on like this, growing bitter, getting thinner, wasting away: he should ask her right away. And Lalo how could he doubt it? He'd ask her, he'd have a girlfriend and he what would I do? and Choto he'd make out and Manny he'd hold her hand and Chingolo he'd kiss her and Lalo he'd fool around with her a little and he and afterwards? and he was losing his voice and they afterwards? and he afterwards, when they had grown up and you get married, and he and you and Lalo: how dumb, how can you think about

that now, and besides that's the least of it. One day he'd
ditch her, he'd start an argument for no reason at all and
he'd fight and so everything would be taken care of and he,
wanting and not wanting to speak: that was just what he
didn't want, because, because he loved her. But a little later
—up to ten beers now—guys, we were right, it was the best
way: I'll ask her to go steady, I'll stay with her awhile and
I'll ditch her.

But the weeks rushed by and we when, P.P., and he
tomorrow, he hadn't made up his mind, he'd ask her tomorrow, honest, suffering as they never saw him suffer
before or after, and the girls "You're wasting time, thinking, thinking," singing the ballad to him "Perhaps, perhaps, perhaps." Then the crisis began for him: all of a
sudden he threw the cue stick down on the floor at the pool
hall, ask her, man! and he started swearing at the bottles or
the cigarette butts, and he tried to pick a fight with anybody
or he burst into tears, tomorrow, this time it was the truth,
on his mother's honor he would: I'll tell her I love her or
I'll kill myself. "And so the days go passing by, and you
despairing . . ." and he would leave the matinee and start
to walk, to trot down Larco Avenue, leave me alone, like a
horse gone crazy, and they behind, go away, he wanted to
be alone, and we ask her, P.P., stop suffering, ask her, ask
her, "Perhaps, perhaps, perhaps." Or he went to the Indian
Messenger and drank, what hatred he felt, Lalo, until he got
drunk, what awful pain. Chotito, and they would accom-
pany him, I feel like killing, man! and we'd half carry him
up to the door of his house, P.P., make up your mind right
now, ask her, and the girls morning and night "For what
you want most, how much longer, how much longer."
They're making his life impossible, we said, he'll end up a
drunk, outlaw, madman.

So the winter ended, another summer began and along with the sun and the heat a boy who studied architecture came to Miraflores from St. Isidor, he had a Pontiac and was a swimmer: Butch Arnilla. He joined the group and at first the guys didn't take to him and the girls what are you doing around here, who invited you, but Terry leave him alone, little white blouse, stop needling him, Butch sit down alongside me, little sailor's hat, blue jeans, I invited him. And they, man, didn't he have eyes in his head? and he sure, he's horning in on your territory, dummy, he's going to take her away from you, get going or your goose'll be cooked, and he so what if he takes her away? and we doesn't matter to you anymore? and he wh-wh-why w-w-would it m-m-matter and they he didn't like her anymore? wh-wh-why w-w-would he l-l-like her.

Butch asked Terry to go steady toward the end of January and she said yes: poor P.P., we said, what a rotten break and about Terry what a flirt, what a bitch, what a dirty trick she played on him. But now the girls stuck up for her: nice work, who was to blame but him, and Chabuca how long was poor Terry going to wait for him to make up his mind? and China what do you mean dirty trick, just the opposite, he played a dirty trick on her, he had her wasting her time for so long and Kitty besides Butch was really friendly, Fina and nice and cute and Chabuca and Cuéllar a scaredy-cat and China a queer.

5.

Then P.P. Cuéllar went back to his old tricks. How crazy, said Lalo, he went surfing during Holy Week? And Chingolo: not just in waves, in mountains of water fifteen feet tall, man, that tall, thirty feet tall. And Choto: they made a

terrible racket, they reached up to the awnings, and
Chabuca farther, to the top of the breakwater, they
splashed the cars on the highway and, of course, nobody
was in the water. Had he done it so Terry Arrarte would see
him? yeah, to make her boyfriend look bad? yeah. For sure,
like telling Terry look what I dare to do and Butch zero, and
he was supposed to be such a great swimmer? he wades
along the shoreline like the women and kids, look who
you've lost, terrific.

Why would the water get so rough during Holy Week?
Fina said, and China in anger because the Jews killed
Christ, and Choto had the Jews killed him? he thought it
was the Romans, how dumb. We were sitting on the breakwater, Fina, in bathing suits, Choto, bare legs, Manny, the
walls of water were crashing, China, and they came right up
and wet our feet, Chabuca, how cold it was, Kitty, and how
dirty, Chingolo, the water black and the foam brown,
Terry, full of seaweed and jellyfish and Butch Arnilla, and
just then psst psst, look, here came Cuéllar. Would he come
over, Terry? would he pretend he didn't see you? He
parked his Ford in front of the Horseshoe jazz club, got out,
went into the Seagulls and came out in bathing trunks—
new ones, said Choto, yellow, Jantzens and Chingolo he
even thought about that, he planned everything to draw
attention, did you catch it, Lalo, a towel around his neck
like a scarf, and sunglasses. He peered scornfully at the
scared swimmers, huddled between the breakwater and the
beach, and looked at the wild and furious walls of water that
washed away the sand and he raised his hand, waved to us
and came over. Hi Cuéllar, some disappointment, huh? hi,
hi, a look like he didn't get it, better if they'd gone swimming at the Regattas pool, wouldn't it? what's new, a look
asking why, how're you? And finally a look of on account

of the big waves? no, how could you think that! what was
wrong with them, what was the matter with us (Kitty: what
goes up's gotta come down, ha ha), if the water was perfect
this way, Terry, little eyes, was he serious? sure, great even
for surfing, he was joking, right? little hands and Butch he'd
dare to ride them? sure, body surfing or with a board,
didn't we believe him? no, that was what we were laughing
about? they were scared? really? and Terry he wasn't? no,
he was going in? yeah, he was going surfing? sure: yelps.
And they saw him throw off his towel, look at Terry Arrarte
(she must have blushed, right? said Lalo, and Choto no,
what was she supposed to do, and Butch? yeah, he shook
like a leaf and run down the steps of the breakwater and
dive into the water head over heels. And we saw him cut
through the undertow along the shoreline and reach the
surf quick as one, two, three. A wave built up and he dived
under and then came up and dived in and came up, what
was he like? a little fish, a porpoise, a yelp, where was he?
another, look at him, part of an arm, there, there. And they
saw him swim out, disappear, appear and grow smaller
until he got out where the breakers started, Lalo, what
breakers: huge, shaking, they rose and never fell, squirm-
ing, was he that little white spot? nerves, yeah. He went out,
came back in, went back out, got lost in the foam and the
waves and slipped back and pushed forward, what did he
look like? a little duck, a little paper boat, and to see him
better Terry stood up, Chabuca, Choto, everybody, even
Butch, but when was he going to ride them? He delayed but
he took heart at last. He turned around toward the beach
and looked for us and waved to us and we waved hello
to him, hello, little towel. He let one, two go by and
with the third breaker they saw him, we imagined him stick
his head under, push off with one arm to find the current,

stiffen his body and kick. He caught it, spread his arms, rose up (a twenty-four-foot wáve? asked Lalo, more, high as the roof? more, like Niagara Falls, then? more, much more) and he fell with the crest of the wave and the mountain of water swallowed him and the big wave appeared, did he get out, did he get out? and it came closer roaring like an airplane, vomiting foam, there, did they see him, was he there? and at last began to drop down, to lose strength and he appeared, so calm, and the wave gently carried him, covered with seaweed, how long he held out without breathing, what lungs, and beached him on the sand, terrific: he had us with our tongues hanging out, Lalo, with good reason, I mean. That was how it started all over again.

Toward the middle of the year, just after the national holiday, Cuéllar started working in his old man's factory: now he'll change, they said, he'll become a serious guy. But it wasn't like that at all, just the opposite. He'd leave the office at six and by seven he'd already be in Miraflores, and by seven-thirty in the Indian Messenger, leaning on the bar, drinking (a boilermaker, miss) and waiting for someone he knew to come in to shoot dice. He would spend the evening there, in the midst of dice, ashtrays full of butts, crapshooters and bottles of cold beer, and he killed the nights seeing a show, in sleazy nightclubs (the National, the Penguin, the Olympic, the Tourbillon) or, if he was broke, ending up getting drunk in the worst dives, where he could pawn his Parker pen, his Omega watch, his gold bracelet (bars in Surquilla or Porvenir), and some mornings he turned up scratched, a black eye, a bandaged hand: he was washed up, we said, and the girls his poor mom and the guys do you know now he hangs out with queers, pimps and junkies? But on Saturdays he always went out with us. He would come around to look for them after lunch and, if we didn't go to the Hippodrome or the stadium, they would shut themselves up at Chingolo's or Manny's to play poker till it got dark. Then we went back home and they showered and we got spruced up and Cuéllar picked them up in the powerful Nash his old man had passed on to him when he came of age, boy, you're already twenty-one, you can vote now and his old lady, sweetheart, don't speed a lot, or one day he was going to kill himself. While we tuned up with a quick drink at the Chinaman's joint on the corner, would they go for Chinese food? gabbing, to Chinatown? and telling jokes, to eat shish-kebab at Under the Bridge? P.P. was a champion, to the pizzeria? do they know the one about and what did the frog say to and the one about the general and if Tony Mella cut himself when he shaved what happened? he castrated himself, ha ha, the poor guy was so ballsy.

After eating, already turned on by the jokes, we went around whoring, barhopping, around Victoria, chattering, on Huanaco Boulevard, downing spicy food, or over on Argentina Avenue, or they'd make a short stop at the Embassy or at the Ambassador to see the first show from the bar and we'd generally end up on Grau Avenue, at Nanette's. The guys from Miraflores got here already, because they knew them there, hi P.P., by their names and by their nicknames, how're you? and the whores nearly died and they too from laughing: he was fine. Cuéllar would get hot under the collar and sometimes he'd tell them off and leave slamming the door, I'm never coming back, but other times he'd laugh and give them free rein and wait, dancing, or seated next to the jukebox with a beer in his hand, or talking to Nanette, let them pick their whore, we went upstairs and they came back down: that was a quickie, Chingolo, he said to them, how was it? or you took your sweet

time, Manny, or I was spying on you through the keyhole,
Choto, you've got hair on your ass, Lalo. And one of those
Saturdays, when they came back into the main room, Cuéllar wasn't there and Nanette all of a sudden he got up, paid
for his beer and left, without even saying good-bye. We
went over to Grau Avenue and found him there, slumped
over the steering wheel of his Nash, trembling, buddy, what
got into you, and Lalo: he was crying. Did you feel bad, old
guy? they asked him, somebody poke fun at you? and
Choto who insulted you? who, they'd go back in and we'd
punch him out and Chingolo, had the whores been bugging
him? and Manny he wasn't going to cry over some dumb
thing like that, was he? Don't pay any attention to them,
P.P., c'mon, don't cry, and he hugged the steering wheel,
sighed and with his head and his cracking voice, no, he
sobbed, no, they hadn't been bugging him, and he wiped
his eyes with his handkerchief, nobody had poked fun,
who'd dare. And they, calm down, man, brother, then why,
too much to drink? no, was he sick? no, nothing, he felt
okay, we slapped him on the back, man, old pal, brother,
they cheered him up, P.P. He should quiet down, laugh,
start up the powerful Nash, let's go somewhere. They'd
have the last round at the Tourbillon, we'll get there just
in time for the second show, P.P., he should get going and
quit crying. Cuéllar finally did calm down, left and by
Twenty-eighth of July Avenue he was already laughing,
man, and suddenly a long face, come clean with us, what
had happened, and he nothing, hell, he just had gotten a
little down, no more, and they how come if life was a bowl
of cherries, pal, and he about a pile of things and Manny,
like what for instance, and he like man offended God so
much for instance, and Lalo what're you talking about? and
Choto he meant they sinned so much? and he yeah, for

instance, some pair of balls, huh? yeah, and also on account of life was so boring. And Chingolo what do you mean it's boring, man, it was a bowl of cherries, and he because you spent your time working, or drinking, or partying, every day the same thing and all of a sudden you were old and died, dumb, isn't it? yeah. Is that what he'd been thinking about at Nanette's? that in front of the whores? yeah, he'd cried over that? yeah, and also out of pity for the poor, for the blind, for cripples, for those panhandlers who begged for charity along the Union strip, and for those newspaper sellers who went around hawking the *Chronicle,* really dumb, isn't it? and for those half-breeds who shine your shoes in Plaza San Martin, some dope, huh? and we: sure, some dope, but he'd gotten over it, right? sure, he'd forgotten about it? sure, c'mon laugh a little, so we can believe you, ha ha. Hurry up, P.P., make it go faster, floor the gas, what time was it, what time did the show start, who knew, would that Cuban mulatto be there forever? what was her name? Ana, what did they call her? the Caymana, c'mon, P.P., show us you got over it, another little laugh: ha ha.

6.

When Lalo married Chabuca, the same year that Manny and Chingolo got their engineering degrees, Cuéllar had already had several accidents and his Volvo went around dented all the time, scratched up, the windows cracked. You're going to kill yourself, sweetheart, don't do crazy things and his old man that was the last straw, boy, how much longer before he changed, out of line once more and he wouldn't give him another cent, he should think it over and mend his ways, if not for yourself for your mother, he

was telling him for his own good. And we: you're too big
to run around with snot-nosed kids, P.P. Because that's
what he had taken to doing. He always spent evenings
shooting craps with the night owls at the Indian Messenger
or D'Onofrio, or gabbing and drinking with queers, with
pushers at the Haiti (when does he work, we'd ask, or is his
working a cock-and-bull story?) but during the day he'd
roam from one section of Miraflores to the next and he was
seen on street corners, gotten up like James Dean (tight
blue jeans, a bright shirt open from the neck to the navel,
a small gold chain dancing on his chest and getting tangled
in the little hairs, white loafers), playing games with the
teen-agers, kicking a ball in a parking lot, playing the guitar. His car was always full of thirteen-, fourteen-, fifteen-
year-old rock 'n' rollers and, on Sundays, he'd turn up at
the Waikiki (make me a member, Dad, surfing was the best
sport for keeping the weight down and he could go there
too, when it was sunny, to have lunch, with the old lady,
next to the ocean) with bunches of kids, get a look at him,
get a look at him, there he is, what a doll, and he came well
escorted, how fresh: one by one he got them up on his
surfboard and he'd go with them out past where the waves
broke. He taught them to drive his Volvo, he'd show off in
front of them by taking curves on two wheels along the
breakwater and he'd bring them to the stadium, to the
wrestling matches, to the bullfights, to the races, to bowling, to boxing. That's that, we said, it was inevitable: fag-
got. And also: what else was left for him, it was understandable, he wasn't to blame but, brother, every day it's harder
to get together with him, they looked at him on the street,
they whistled at him and pointed him out, and Choto you're
really concerned about what they'll say, and Manny they'd
bad mouth him and Lalo if they see us with him a lot and

Chingolo they'll get the wrong idea about you.

He put some time into sports and they he does it more than anything else to draw attention: P.P. Cuéllar, car racer like he used to be of waves. He took part in the Atocongo Circuit and came in third. His picture was in the *Chronicle* and in the *Commerce* congratulating the winner, Arnaldo Alvarado was the best said Cuéllar, the good loser. But he became even more famous a little later on, betting on a race at dawn, from Plaza San Martin to Salazar Park, with Kiki Ganoza, the latter in the proper lane, P.P. against the traffic. The highway patrol chased him from Javier Prado Street, they only caught up with him at Second of May Street, how fast he must have been going. He spent a day at police headquarters and that's it? we asked, with this scandal will he learn his lesson and shape up? But in a few weeks he had his first serious accident, doing the pass of death—his hands tied to the steering wheel, his eyes blindfolded—on Angamos Avenue. And the second, three months later, the night we gave Lalo his bachelor party. Enough, quit playing kids' games, said Chingolo, stop right now since they were too big for these kids' pranks and we wanted to get out. But he don't even try, what was eating us, no confidence in the pro? such great big men and so scared, don't piss your pants, where was a muddy corner to take a slippery curve? He was wild and they couldn't convince him, Cuéllar, buddy, it's okay, leave us off at our houses, and Lalo he was getting married tomorrow, he didn't want to break his neck the night before, don't be so inconsiderate, he shouldn't go up on the sidewalk, don't run the light at that speed, stop being a pain. He hit a taxi on Alcanfores and Lalo he wasn't hurt, but Manny and Choto bruised their faces and he broke three ribs. We had a falling out and a little later he telephoned them and we made up and they went out to eat together but this time something had come between them and him and it was never the same again.

From then on we didn't see much of each other and when Manny got married he sent him an announcement of the wedding without an invitation, and he didn't go to the bachelor party and when Chingolo came back from the United States married to a pretty Yankee and with two kids who hardly spoke a word of Spanish, Cuéllar had already gone up into the mountains, to Tingo Maria, to grow coffee, they said, and whenever he came down into Lima and they met him on the street, we hardly said hello, what's new kid, how are you P.P., what's up old boy, so-so, ciao, and he had already come back to Miraflores, crazier than ever, and he had already killed himself, going up north, how? in a crack-up, where? on those treacherous curves at Pasamayo, poor guy, we said at the funeral, how much he suffered, what a life he had, but this finish is something he had in store for him.

They were mature and settled men by now and we all had a wife, car, children who studied at Champagnat, Immaculate Conception or St. Mary's, and they were building themselves a little summerhouse in Ancon, St. Rose or the beaches in the south, and we began to get fat and to have gray hair, potbellies, soft bodies, to wear reading glasses, to feel uneasy after eating and drinking and age spots already showed up on their skin as well as certain wrinkles.

The Leaders

1.

Javier jumped the gun by a split second.

"The whistle!" he shouted, already up on his feet.

The tension broke, violently, like an explosion. We were all standing up. Dr. Abasolo's mouth was open. He turned red, clenching his fists. When he raised his hand and, getting a grip on himself, seemed on the verge of launching into a sermon, the whistle really did blow. We ran out in an uproar, frenzied, urged on by the crow's cackle from Amaya, who pushed ahead turning over desks.

Yells jolted the courtyard. The third- and fourth-year students had gotten out earlier: they formed a huge circle that swirled beneath the dust. The first and second years came out almost at the same time we did: they brought new, aggressive phrases, more hatred. The circle grew. Indignation was unanimous in the high school. (The elementary school had a small blue mosaic patio in the opposite wing of the building.)

"He wants to screw us, the hick."

"Yeah, up his."

Nobody said a word about final exams. The students' excitement, the shouting, the commotion, all pointed to this as the right time for confronting the principal. Suddenly I stopped trying to hold myself back and I feverishly started running from group to group. "He picks on us and we don't say a word?" "We've got to do something." "We've got to do something *to him.*"

An iron hand yanked me out of the center of the circle. "Not you," said Javier. "Don't get mixed up in this. They'll expel you. You know that already."

"Doesn't matter to me now. I'm going to make him pay for everything. It's my chance, see? Let's get them into formation."

We went around the courtyard whispering in each ear: "Get in line." "Form ranks, on the double."

"Let's line up!" Raygada's booming voice vibrated in the suffocating morning air.

A lot of the others chimed in:

"Ranks! Ranks!"

Surprised, the school monitors Gallardo and Romero then saw that the uproar had suddenly subsided and that the ranks were formed before recess was over. Watching us nervously, they were leaning against the wall next to the teachers' lounge. Then they looked at each other. In the doorway several teachers had appeared: they too were surprised.

Gallardo came over.

"Listen!" he shouted, confused. "We still haven't—"

"Shut up," somebody snapped back from the rear. "Shut up, Gallardo, you queer!"

Gallardo grew pale. With long strides, with a threatening gesture, he invaded the rows. Behind his back, several students yelled, "Gallardo's a queer!"

"Let's march," I said. "Let's go round the courtyard. Seniors lead off."

We started marching, stomping vigorously, until it hurt our feet. On the second time around—we formed a perfect rectangle, in line with the contours of the courtyard— Javier, Raygada, Leon and I started in:

"Sche-dule; sche-dule; sche-dule . . ."

Everybody joined in the chorus.

"Louder!" burst out the voice of someone I hated: Lou. "Shout!"

Immediately the din rose until it was deafening.

"Sche-dule; sche-dule; sche-dule . . ."

Cautiously, the teachers had disappeared, closing the door to the lounge behind them. When the seniors passed the corner where Teobaldo was selling fruit on a plank, he said something we didn't catch. He moved his hands, as if cheering us on. Pig, I thought.

The shouting got stronger. But neither the rhythm of the march nor the stimulus of the shrieking were enough to hide our fear. The wait was nerve-racking. Why did he delay coming out? Still feigning courage, we repeated the chant, but they had begun to look at each other and from time to time little laughs, sharp and forced, could be heard. "I mustn't think about anything," I said to myself. "Not now." By this time it was hard for me to shout: I was hoarse and my throat burned. Suddenly, almost without realizing it, I looked at the sky: I was following a buzzard that glided gently over the school, under a big, blue dome, clear and deep, lit up by a yellow disk like a blemish on one side. I lowered my head quickly.

Small and livid, Ferrufino had appeared at the end of a corridor that led out into the recess grounds. His short, bowlegged steps, like a duck's, brought him closer, harshly breaking the silence that suddenly reigned, surprising me. (The door of the teachers' lounge opens: a dwarfish, comic face peeps out. Estrada wants to get a look at us; he sees the principal a few steps away; he vanishes swiftly; his childish hand closes the door.) Ferrufino was facing us: he roamed wild-eyed through the groups of silenced students. The ranks had broken: some ran to the lavatories, others desperately encircled Teobaldo's stand. Javier, Raygada, Leon and I stood motionless.

"Don't be afraid," I said, but nobody heard me because the principal had said at the very same time:

"Blow the whistle, Gallardo."

Again the rows formed, this time slowly. The heat was not unbearable yet, but we were already suffering from a certain drowsiness, a kind of boredom. "They got tired," Javier murmured. "That's bad." And, furious, he warned:

"Careful about talking."

Others spread the warning.

"No," I said. "Wait. They'll go wild the minute Ferrufino opens his mouth."

Several seconds of silence, of suspicious seriousness, went by before we raised our eyes, one by one, toward that little man dressed in gray. He stood there with his hands clasped over his belly, his feet together, perfectly still.

"I don't want to know who started this commotion," he recited. An actor: the tone of his voice, measured, smooth, the almost cordial words, his pose like a statue's, were all carefully calculated. Could he have been rehearsing all by himself in his office? "Actions like this are a disgrace to you, to the school and to me. I've been very patient, too patient —mark my words—with the instigator of these disruptions, but this is the limit. . . ."

Me or Lou? An endless and greedy tongue of fire licked

my back, my shoulders, my cheeks, at the same time that the
eyes of everyone in the school turned in my direction. Was
Lou looking at me? Was he envious? Were the Coyotes
looking at me? From behind, someone patted my arm
twice, encouraging me. The principal spoke for a long time
about God, about discipline and the supreme values of the
spirit. He said that the administration's doors were always
open, that the truly courageous should come in to face up
to the consequences.

"To face the consequences," he repeated: now he was
authoritarian. "That is, to talk face to face with me."

"Don't be a sucker!" I said quickly. "Don't be a sucker!"

But he'd already raised his hand when Ferrufino saw him
take a step to the left, breaking ranks. A satisfied smile
crossed Ferrufino's mouth and vanished immediately.

"I'm listening, Raygada . . ." he said.

As Raygada spoke, his words gave him courage. He even
managed, at one moment, to wave his arms dramatically.
He asserted that we weren't bad and that we loved the
school and our teachers; he reminded him that youth was
impulsive. In the name of all of us, he asked for pardon.
Then he stammered but went on:

"We ask you, Mr. Principal, to post an exam schedule as
in past years. . . ." Frightened, he grew silent.

"Take note, Gallardo," said Ferrufino. "The student
Raygada will come to study next week, every day, until nine
at night." He paused. "The reason will go down on your
report card: rebelling against a pedagogical decree."

"Mr. Principal . . ." Raygada was livid.

"Seems fair to me," whispered Javier. "Serves him
right."

2.

A ray of sunlight pierced the dirty skylight and ended up caressing my forehead and eyes, filling me with peace. Still, my heart beat faster than usual and at times I felt short of breath. A half hour was left before dismissal; the boys' impatience had settled down a little. Would they respond after all?

"Sit down, Montes," said Professor Zambrano. "You're an ass."

"Nobody doubts that," asserted Javier, right beside me. "He is an ass."

Could the rallying cry have reached every grade? I didn't want to torment my brain all over again with pessimistic assumptions, but I had my eye on Lou a few feet away from my desk, and I felt anxious and doubtful, because deep down I knew that what was at stake was not the exam schedule, not even a question of honor, but a personal vendetta. Why give up this lucky chance to attack the enemy when he'd dropped his guard?

"Here," somebody next to me said. "It's from Lou."

I accept taking command, with you and Raygada. Lou had signed twice. Between his signatures, like a small blot with the ink still shining, there appeared a sign we all respected: the letter C, upper case, enclosed in a black circle. I looked over at him: his forehead and mouth were pinched; he had slanted eyes, sunken cheeks and a strong, pronounced jaw. He was watching me intently: maybe he thought the situation required him to be cordial.

I answered on the same piece of paper: *With Javier.* He read without shifting and shook his head yes.

"Javier," I said.

"I know," he answered. "Okay. We'll give him a rough time."

Give who? The principal or Lou? I was just about to ask him but the whistle for the end of the period distracted me. At the same time, the shouting rose over our heads, mixed with the noise of pushed desks. Someone—Cordoba maybe?—whistled loudly as if trying to stand out.

"They know already?" Raygada asked, on line. "To the embankment."

"What a fast thinker!" somebody called out. "Even Ferrufino knows."

We went out the back door fifteen minutes ahead of the lower grades. Others had left already and most of the students had stopped in the street, forming small groups. They were talking, fooling around, shoving each other.

"Nobody hang around here," I said.

"The Coyotes with me," Lou shouted proudly.

Twenty boys surrounded him.

"To the embankment," he ordered. "Everybody to the embankment."

Arm in arm in a row linking the two sidewalks, the seniors brought up the rear, elbowing our way through, forcing the less enthusiastic ones to speed up:

A cool breeze that could not even stir the dry leaves of the carob trees or the hair on our heads blew the sand from one side of the embankment to the other, covering the burning hot surface. They had responded. Before us—Lou, Javier, Raygada and I, with our backs to the railing and the endless dunes stretching from the opposite bank of the river—a packed crowd extending the length of the whole block remained quiet, even though from time to time strident, isolated shouts could be heard.

"Who does the talking?" Javier asked.

"I will," proposed Lou, ready to jump up on the railing.
"No," I said. "Javier, you speak."

Lou checked himself and looked at me, but he wasn't mad.

"All right," he said, and shrugging his shoulders, added: "What's the difference?"

Javier climbed up. With one hand he leaned on a twisted, dry tree and with the other he held himself up on my neck. Through his legs, agitated by a slight quivering that disappeared as the tone of his voice grew convincing and forceful, I could see the dry, burning riverbed and thought about Lou and about the Coyotes. A mere second had been enough for him to take over. Now he was in command and they looked up to him, him, a little yellow rat who not six months earlier had been begging me to let him join the gang. The tiniest slip, and then blood pouring down my face and neck; and my arms and legs, immobilized beneath the moon's brightness, unable now to answer back to his fists.

"I beat you," he said, panting. "Now I'm the leader. Let's get that settled."

None of the shadows spread out in a circle over the soft sand had moved. Only the frogs and crickets answered Lou, who was insulting me. Still stretched out on the hot ground, I managed to yell out:

"I'm quitting the gang. I'll start another one, better than this one."

But I and Lou and the Coyotes still crouched in the shadows knew it wasn't true.

"I'm quitting too," said Javier.

He helped me get up. We went back into town and while we were walking through the empty streets, I was wiping away the blood and tears with Javier's handkerchief.

"Now you talk," said Javier. He had got down and some of them were applauding him.

"Okay," I answered and got up on the railing.

Neither the walls in the background nor the bodies of my pals cast shadows. My palms were moist and I thought it was nerves, but it was the heat. The sun was in the center of the sky; it was suffocating. My buddies' eyes didn't meet mine: they looked at the ground or my knees. They kept quiet. The sun protected me. "We'll ask the principal to post the exam schedule, just the same as other years. Raygada, Javier, Lou and I will make up the committee. Junior high agrees, right?"

Most agreed, nodding their heads. A few shouted, "Yes."

"We'll do it right now," I said. "You'll wait for us at Merino Square."

We started walking. The main door to the school was shut. We knocked loudly; behind us we heard a growing murmur. Gallardo opened up.

"Are you crazy?" he asked. "Don't do this."

"Don't get mixed up in it," Lou interrupted him. "Do you think a hick scares us?"

"Go in," Gallardo said. "You'll see."

3.

His little eyes observed us closely. He tried to feign irony and a lack of concern, but we knew that his smile was forced and that deep inside his thick-set body were fear and hatred. He knitted his brow and wiped away his scowl as sweat gushed out of his small, purple hands.

He was shaking.

"Do you know what this is called? It's called rebellion, insurrection. Do you think I'm going to submit myself to the whims of a few idlers? I'll crush your insolence. . . ."

He lowered and raised his voice. I saw him fight not to shout. Why don't you explode once and for all, I thought. Coward!

He had stood up. A gray smudge floated around his hands, which rested on his glass-topped desk. Suddenly his voice rose, grew harsh.

"Get out! Whoever mentions exams again will be duly punished."

Before Javier or I could make a signal to him, the real Lou showed himself: the nighttime raider of filthy huts in Tablada, the fighter of the Wolves in the dunes.

"Sir . . ."

I didn't turn to look at him. His slanting eyes must have been shooting sparks of fire and fury, as when we fought on the dry riverbed. Now, too, he must have had his mouth open, filled with spit, baring his yellow teeth.

"Neither can we accept their flunking us all because you don't want any schedules. Why do you want us all to get bad grades? Why? . . ."

Ferrufino had come close. He nearly touched him with his body. Pale, terrified, Lou continued to speak:

"We're sick and tired of—"

"Shut up!"

The principal had raised his arms and his fists clenched something.

"Shut up!" he repeated angrily. "Shut up, you animal! How dare you!"

Lou was already silent, but he looked Ferrufino in the eyes as if he were suddenly going to lunge at his neck. They're just alike, I thought: Two dogs.

"So, you've learned from this one."

His finger was pointing at my forehead. I bit my lip: soon

I felt a thin, hot thread coursing along my tongue and that calmed me.

"Get out!" he shouted again. "Get out of here! You'll regret this."

We left. A motionless and gasping crowd sprawled right up to the edge of the steps connecting San Miguel School to Merino Square. Our schoolmates had invaded the small gardens and the fountain: they were mute and anxious. Oddly, in the midst of the bright, static patch appeared small white rectangles that no one stepped on. The heads seemed identical, uniform, as in parade formation. We crossed the square. No one questioned us: they moved to one side, making way for us, with tight lips. Until we stepped out onto the street they held their place. Then, following a signal none of us had given, they walked behind us, out of step, just as they did when walking to class.

The pavement was boiling: it looked like a mirror melting in the sunlight. Can it be true? I thought. One hot, deserted night they told me about it, on this same street, and I didn't believe it. But the newspapers said that in some faraway places the sun drove men crazy and sometimes killed them.

"Javier," I asked, "you saw the egg fry all by itself on the street?"

Surprised, he shook his head. "No. They told me about it."

"Can it be true?"

"Maybe. We could test it now. The ground's burning up; like hot coals."

Albert appeared in the doorway of the Queen. His blond hair shone wonderfully: it looked like gold. Friendly, he waved his right hand. His enormous green eyes were wide open and he smiled. He must have been wondering where

this uniformed and silent crowd was marching to in the
brutal heat.

"Coming back later?" he called to me.

"Can't. See you tonight."

"He's an idiot," said Javier. "He's a drunk."

"No," I asserted. "He's my friend. He's a nice guy."

4.

"Let me talk, Lou," I asked him, trying to keep cool.

But nobody could contain him now. He was standing up
on the railing, under the branches of the withered carob
tree: he held his balance admirably and his skin and face
reminded you of a lizard.

"No!" he said aggressively. "*I'm* going to talk."

I signaled to Javier. We went up to Lou and grabbed his
legs. But he managed to grab hold of the tree in time and
wriggle his right leg out of my arms. Driven back three
steps by a strong kick in the shoulder, I saw Javier quickly
seize Lou by the knees and raise his face defiantly with eyes
scorched by the sun.

"Don't hit him!" I shouted. He restrained himself, shaking, while Lou began to scream:

"Know what the principal told us? He insulted us, he
treated us like dogs. He doesn't feel like posting the
schedules because he wants to make it hard on us. He'll
flunk the whole school and it doesn't matter to him. He's
a . . ."

We were back at the starting point and the twisted rows
of boys started swaying. Nearly the entire junior high was
still there. With the heat and each word from Lou, the
students' resentment grew. They were incensed.

"We know he hates us. We don't get along with him.

Since he arrived, this school isn't a school. He insults us, he whips us. On top of everything else, he wants to screw us on the exams."

A sharp, anonymous voice interrupted him:

"Who's he whipped?"

Lou hesitated for a second. He exploded all over again. "Who?" he challenged. "Arévalo! Show them your back!"

Amid whispers, Arévalo emerged from the center of the crowd, pale. He was a Coyote. He went up to Lou and uncovered his chest and back. A thick red welt showed on his ribs.

"This is Ferrufino!" Lou's hand pointed to the mark while his eyes studied the astonished faces of those nearby. Tumultuously the human sea pressed around us: everyone struggled to get close to Arévalo and nobody listened to Lou or to Javier and Raygada, who were asking for calm, nor to me, shouting: "It's a lie! Don't pay any attention to him! It's a lie!" The tide carried me away from the railing and from Lou. I was suffocating. I managed to open a path for myself until I got out of the mob. I loosened my tie and slowly caught my breath with my mouth open and my arms straight up, until I felt my heart regain its beat.

Raygada was next to me. Indignant, he asked me:

"When did that happen to Arévalo?"

"Never."

"What?"

Even he, always calm, had been taken in. His nostrils were quivering sharply and he was squeezing his fists together.

"Nothing," I said. "I don't know when it was."

Lou waited for the excitement to die down a little. Then, raising his voice over the scattered complaints:

"Is Ferrufino going to beat us?" he shouted, his angry fist threatening the students. "Is he going to beat us? Answer me!"

"No!" five hundred or more burst out. "No! No!"

Shaken by the effort his shrieking had required of him, Lou was swaying victoriously on the railing.

"Nobody goes into the school until the exam schedule's posted. That's only fair. It's our right. And we won't let anyone enter the elementary school either."

His aggressive voice got lost in the shouting. In front of me, in the bristling crowd of raised arms jubilantly throwing hundreds of caps into the air, I couldn't make out a single one who remained indifferent or opposed.

"What're we going to do?" Javier wanted to look calm, but his eyes glittered.

"It's okay," I said. "Lou's right. Let's help him."

I ran to the railing and climbed up. "Tell the kids in the lower grades there's no afternoon classes," I said. "They can go home now. Kids in the upper classes stay to surround the school."

"And the Coyotes too," Lou finished, happy.

5.

"I'm hungry," Javier said.

The heat had let up. On the one usable bench in Merino Square we were taking the sun's rays, gently filtered through a few clouds that had appeared in the sky, but almost nobody was sweating.

Leon rubbed his hands together and smiled. He was fidgety.

"Don't tremble," said Amaya. "You're too big to be afraid of Ferrufino."

"Watch it!" Leon's monkey face had gone red and his chin stuck out. "Watch it, Amaya!" He was up on his feet.

"Don't fight," Raygada said calmly. "Nobody's scared. You'd have to be a screwball."

"Let's go around the back way," Javier suggested.

We went around the school, walking down the middle of the street. The high windows were half open and you couldn't see anyone behind them or hear any sound.

"They're eating lunch," Javier said.

"Yeah. Of course."

The main door of the Catholic school towered over the sidewalk across the street. Boarders were posted up on the roof, observing us. Undoubtedly, they'd been informed.

"What brave guys!" somebody jeered.

Javier gibed at them. A shower of threats was the response. Some of them spat, but missed. There was laughter. "They're dying of envy," Javier whispered.

At the corner we saw Lou. He was sitting on the sidewalk, all alone and looking distractedly at the street. He saw us and came over. He was happy.

"Two brats from the first year came," he said. "We sent them down to the river to play."

"Yeah?" said Javier. "Wait half an hour and you'll see. There's going to be fireworks."

Lou and the Coyotes guarded the back door of the school. They were spread out between the corners of Lima and Arequipa streets. When we got to the entrance to the alley, they were talking in a huddle and laughing. All of them were carrying sticks and stones.

"Not that way," I said. "If you hit them, the brats are going to want to get in anyhow."

Lou laughed. "You'll see. Nobody gets in through this door."

He too had a club, which he had hidden behind his body until then. He showed us, waving it.

"And over there?" he asked.

"Nothing yet."

Behind us someone shouted our names. It was Raygada: he came running toward us calling, waving excitedly. "They're coming, they're coming," he said anxiously. "Come on." Suddenly he stopped ten yards short of reaching us. He turned on his heels and went back at a full run. He was very excited. Javier and I ran too. Lou shouted something to us about the river. The river? I thought. There isn't any. Why does everybody talk about the river if water flows only one month a year? Javier was running at my side, puffing.

"Can we hold them back?"

"What?" It was hard for him to open his mouth. He was tired out.

"Can we hold back the lower grades?"

"I think so. All depends."

"Look."

In the center of the square, next to the fountain, Leon, Amaya and Raygada were talking with a group of little kids, five or six of them. The situation seemed calm.

"I repeat"—Raygada was panting—"go down to the river. There's no class, there's no class. Is that clear? Or do I have to paint you a picture?"

"You do that," said one with a snub nose. "In color."

"Look here," I said to them. "Today nobody's going into school. Let's go down to the river. We'll play soccer: elementary against junior high. Okay?"

"Ha ha." The one with the nose laughed, cocksure. "We'll beat them. There's more of us."

"We'll see. Get down there."

"I don't want to," said one daring voice. "I'm going to school."

He was a boy in the elementary school, thin and pale. His long neck rose out of his commando shirt, which was too big for him, like a broomstick. He was the monitor for his year. Unsure of his own boldness, he took a few steps backward. Leon ran and grabbed him by the arm.

"Didn't you understand?" He had pushed his face into the boy's and was shouting at him. What the hell was Leon so scared about? "Didn't you understand, kid? Nobody's going in. Now move, get going."

"Don't push," I said. "He'll go by himself."

"I'm not going!" he shouted. His face raised to Leon, he looked up at him furiously. "I'm not going! I'm against the strike!"

"Shut up, you birdbrain! What strike?" Leon seemed very nervous. He squeezed the monitor's arm with all his strength. Amused, his companions watched the scene.

"They can expel us!" the monitor yelled at the little kids, showing his fear and anger. "They want a strike because they're not going to give them an exam schedule, they're going to spring the exams on them without their knowing when. Think I don't know? They can expel us! Let's go to school, guys!"

There was a surprised movement among the young boys. They exchanged glances without smiling now, while the monitor went on screaming that they were going to be expelled. He cried.

"Don't hit him!" I shouted, too late. Leon had hit him in the face, not very hard, but the kid had begun to kick and wail.

"You're acting like a baby," somebody observed.

I looked at Javier. He'd already run over. He picked up

the kid and tossed him over his shoulder like a bundle. He
went off with him. Several of the boys followed, laughing
loudly.

"To the river!" Raygada shouted. Javier heard, because
we saw him turn with his load on Sanchez Cerro Street,
headed for the embankment.

The cluster around us was growing: some were sitting on
the fences and the broken benches, others strolling wearily
along the narrow asphalt paths in the park, and no one,
fortunately, was trying to get into school. Scattered in pairs,
the ten boys in charge of guarding the main door tried to
incite them: "They've got to post schedules because if they
don't, they're screwing us. And you too, when it's your
turn."

"They're still arriving," Raygada told me. "We're just a
handful. They can smash us if they want."

"If we keep them busy for ten minutes, it'll be all over,"
said Leon. "The junior high will get here and then we'll
herd them down to the river."

Suddenly one boy shouted in a frenzy: "They're right!
They're right!" And addressing us with a dramatic air: "I'm
with you."

"Great! Terrific!" We applauded him. "You're a real
man."

We slapped him on the back and hugged him.

His example spread. Somebody let out a yell: "Me too."
"You're right." They began to argue among themselves.
We encouraged the more excited ones, flattering them.
"Good, kid. You're no pansy."

Raygada climbed up on the fountain. He had his cap in
his right hand and was waving it gently.

"Let's come to an agreement," he cried out. "Everybody
together?"

They surrounded him. Groups of students continued to arrive, some from the upper grades of the junior high. As Raygada spoke, we formed a wall with them, stretching between the fountain and the school door.

"This is what I call solidarity," he was saying. "Solidarity." He fell silent as if he had finished, but a second later he spread his arms and roared: "We won't allow them to get away with injustice!"

They applauded him.

"Let's go down to the river," I said. "Everybody."

"Okay. You too."

"We'll go afterwards."

"All of us together or nobody," replied the same voice. Nobody moved.

Javier returned. He was alone.

"Those kids are calm," he said. "They've taken a donkey away from some lady. They're having a great time playing."

"The time," Leon asked. "Somebody tell me what time it is."

It was two o'clock.

"We'll leave at two-thirty," I said. "Only one guy has to stay here to warn the latecomers."

Those who were arriving merged with the crowd of kids. They were easily convinced.

"It's dangerous," Javier said. He spoke in a strange manner: could he be afraid? "It's dangerous. We already know what's going to happen if the principal gets it into his head to come out here. Before he opens his mouth, we'll all be in class."

"Yeah," I replied. "They should get going. We've got to stir them up."

But nobody wanted to move. There was tension. From

one moment to the next, everybody expected something to happen. Leon was at my side.

"The junior high kids have carried out their orders," he said. "Look. Only the ones in charge of the doors have come."

Scarcely a moment later, we saw the junior high students arrive in large clusters which mixed in with the waves of kids. They were cracking jokes. Javier became furious.

"And you guys?" he asked. "What're you doing here? Why did you come?"

He was addressing those closest to us. At their head was Antenor, brigadier of the second year in junior high.

"Huh?" Antenor seemed very surprised. "You think we'd go in? We came to help."

Javier leaped at him, grabbed him by the neck.

"Help us! What about your uniforms? And your books?"

"Shut up!" I said. "Let him go. No fights. In ten minutes we're going down to the river. Almost the whole school's come."

The square was completely filled. The students remained quiet; there were no arguments. Some were smoking. A lot of cars were going by on Sanchez Cerro Street and they slowed down crossing Merino Square. From a truck, a man hailed us, shouting:

"Good going, boys. Give 'em hell."

"See?" said Javier. "The whole city knows. Can you picture Ferrufino's face?"

"Two-thirty!" Leon shouted. "Let's go. Quick."

I looked at my watch: five minutes left.

"C'mon!" I shouted. "Let's go down to the river."

Some made as if to move. Javier, Leon, Raygada and several others also shouted and they started pushing one or another of the students. A single word was repeated without letup: "River, river, river."

Slowly, the crowd of students started getting roused. We stopped spurring them on and when we became quiet, I was surprised for the second time that day: total silence. I felt myself getting nervous. I broke the silence.

"Junior high at the back," I indicated. "At the end, lining up . . ."

Next to me somebody threw an ice cream cone to the ground and it splattered my shoes. Joining our arms, we formed a human cordon. We were advancing laboriously. No one was holding back, but the march was very slow. A head was nearly buried in my chest. He turned around: what was his name? His small eyes were friendly.

"Your father'll kill you," he said.

Oh, I thought. My neighbor. "No," I answered. "Well, we'll see. Push on."

We had left the square. The broad column completely filled the breadth of the avenue. Two blocks farther up, above the hatless heads, you could see the yellow-green railing and the huge carob trees along the embankment. Between them, like tiny white dots, the dunes.

The first to hear was Javier, who was marching next to me. There was alarm in his dark, narrow eyes.

"What's going on?" I asked. "Tell me."

He shook his head.

"What's going on?" I shouted. "What do you hear?"

At that instant I managed to see a uniformed boy who was crossing Merino Square toward us in a hurry. The shouts of the recent arrival mingled in my ears with the violent uproar that broke loose as if in confusion from the tight column of boys. Those of us who marched at the end of the line didn't understand very well. We were bewildered for a moment: we unlinked our arms; some freed themselves. We felt ourselves hurled backward, separated. Hundreds of bodies were passing over us, running and shouting hysterically. "What's happening?" I shouted to Leon. With his finger he pointed at something, without ceasing to run. "It's Lou," I heard them whispering. "Something's happened over there. They say it's a mess."

I broke into a run.

At the intersection a few yards from the school's rear door, I stopped short. At that moment it was impossible to see: waves of uniforms poured in from every side and covered the street with shouts and bare heads. Suddenly, about fifteen feet ahead, I caught a glimpse of Lou perched on top of something. His thin body was outlined clearly in the shadow of the wall that held him up. Then, in the din, louder than the voices of the boys insulting him and retreating in order to avoid his fists, I heard his voice:

"Who's gonna try getting near?" he was shouting. "Who's gonna try getting near?"

Four yards away two Coyotes, also surrounded, were defending themselves with sticks and desperately trying to break through the circle and join Lou. Among those in pursuit, I saw faces from the junior high. Some had picked up rocks and were throwing them, although without coming close. At the same time I saw in the distance two other gang members who were running away terrified: a group of boys with sticks chased them.

"Calm down! Calm down! Let's get to the river." A voice full of distress rose up beside me. It was Raygada. He seemed about to cry.

"Don't be an idiot," said Javier. He was laughing loudly. "Shut up, can't you see?"

The door was open and students were eagerly rushing through it by the dozen. More schoolmates continued to arrive at the intersection; some joined the group surrounding Lou and his followers. They had managed to unite. Lou had his shirt open: you could see his thin, hairless chest, sweaty and shiny. A thread of blood trickled from his nose and lips. From time to time he would spit and he looked with hatred at the boys nearest him. He alone kept his stick raised, ready to crash it down. Exhausted, the others had lowered theirs.

"Who's gonna try getting near? I want to see the face on that hero."

As they were entering the school, they were putting their caps and class badges on, any which way. The group surrounding Lou was disintegrating little by little.

Raygada nudged me. "He said he could beat the whole school with his gang." He spoke sadly. "Why did we leave that numbskull alone?"

Raygada went off. From the door he signaled to us, as if in doubt. Then he went in. Javier and I went up to Lou. He was trembling with rage.

"Why didn't you guys come?" he asked, frantic, raising his voice. "Why didn't you come to help us? There were only eight of us, because the others . . ."

He had a sharp eye and was as lithe as a cat. He quickly ducked backward as my fist barely grazed his ear and then, with the weight of his whole body, he swung his club in the air. I took the blow on my chest and reeled. Javier slipped between us.

"Not here," he said. "Let's go to the embankment."

"Let's go," said Lou. "I'm going to teach you all over again."

"We'll see," I answered. "Let's go."

We walked half a block, slowly, because my legs were unsteady. On the corner Leon stopped us.

"Don't fight," he said. "It's not worth it. Let's go to school. We have to be united."

Lou squinted at me. He seemed embarrassed.

"Why did you swing at the kids?" I asked him. "Know what's going to happen to you and me now?"

He didn't answer or make any gesture. He had calmed down completely and his head was lowered.

"Answer me, Lou," I insisted. "Do you know?"

"It's okay," said Leon. "We'll try to help you out. Shake hands."

Apparently sorry, Lou raised his face and looked at me. When I felt his hand in mine, I realized that it was soft and delicate, and that this was the first time we'd greeted each other this way. We swung around and walked Indian file, toward the school. I felt an arm on my shoulder. It was Javier.

The Grandfather

Each time a twig cracked or a frog croaked or the window-panes rattled in the kitchen at the back of the garden, the old man jumped spryly from his improvised seat on a flat rock and spied anxiously through the foliage. But the boy still had not appeared. Through the dining room windows opening onto the pergola he saw, instead, the beams from the chandelier lit some time ago and below them moving shadows that slithered from one side to the other with the curtains, slowly. Ever since he was a boy, he had been nearsighted, so his efforts were futile in trying to determine whether they were eating already or if those restless shadows came from the tallest trees.

He went back to his seat and waited. The previous night it had rained and the ground and flowers gave off a pleasant odor of dampness. But the insects were teeming; and waving his hands around his head desperately, Don Eulogio still did not succeed in chasing them away: every second, invisible lances managed to sting the flesh of his trembling chin, his forehead and even the hollows around his eyes. The enthusiasm and excitement that had kept him ready and feverish during the day had dwindled and now he felt tired and a little sad. He was cold, the darkness of the huge garden bothered him and he was tormented by the persistent, humiliating image of someone—maybe the cook or perhaps the butler—suddenly surprising him in his hiding place. "Don Eulogio, what are you doing out here in the garden at this time of night?" And his son and son-in-law would come, convinced that he was crazy. Trembling nervously, he turned his head and divined the narrow path that led, between the clumps of chrysanthemums, spikenard and roses, up to the back door, skirting the pigeon house. It hardly even calmed him to recall that he had checked three times to make sure that the door was shut, its latch undone, and that in a few seconds he could escape out onto the street without being seen.

And what if he's already come? he thought nervously. Because there had been a second, a few minutes, after he had stealthily gotten into his house by way of the nearly forgotten entry through the garden, when he lost his sense of time and remained as if asleep. He only reacted when the object he was stroking now without realizing it fell out of his hands and struck his thigh. But it was impossible. The boy could not have crossed the garden yet, because his frightened footsteps would have awakened the old man, or the little boy would have shouted when he made out his grandfather, hunched over and sleeping, right at the edge of the path that should lead him to the kitchen.

This thought cheered him. The wind had died down, his body was growing accustomed to the surroundings, he had stopped trembling. Groping in the pockets of his jacket, he found the hard, cylindrical body of the candle he had bought that afternoon at the corner store. Delighted, the old man smiled in the dark: he recalled the saleswoman's surprised expression. He had stood quite serious, tapping his heel quite elegantly, beating his long, metal-plated cane softly and in a circle, while the woman passed different-sized tapers and candles under his eyes. "That one," he said with a rapid gesture meant to indicate annoyance with the disagreeable task he was carrying out. The saleswoman insisted on wrapping it, but Don Eulogio refused and left the store hastily. For the rest of the afternoon he was at the National Club, shut up in the small card room, where nobody ever came. Still, carrying to an extreme his precautions for avoiding the waiters' attentiveness, he locked the door. Then, comfortably sunk into the scarlet armchair, he opened the briefcase he had carried with him and took out the precious package. He had wrapped it in his beautiful white silk scarf, exactly the same one he was wearing the afternoon of the discovery.

At the most ashen hour of dusk he had taken a taxi, telling the driver to drive around the outskirts of the city: a delicious, cool breeze was blowing, and the sight of the sky, between grayish and reddish, would be more mysterious in the middle of the countryside. While the car sailed smoothly over the asphalt, the aged man's lively little eyes —the only active signs in his flaccid face, sunk in bags— slipped distractedly along the edge of the canal running parallel to the highway, and suddenly he sighted it.

"Pull over!" he said, but the driver did not hear him. "Pull over! Stop!" When the car stopped and backed up to the mound of rocks, Don Eulogio verified that it was, in fact, a skull. Holding it between his hands, he forgot the breeze and the countryside and with growing anxiousness minutely studied that hard, unyielding, hostile and impenetrable form, stripped of flesh and skin, with no nose, no eyes, no tongue. It was small and he felt inclined to think it was a child's. It was dirty, dusty, and its bare cranium was punctured by a coin-size opening with splintered edges. The nasal orifice was a perfect triangle, separated from the mouth by a thin bridge not quite so yellow as the chin. He amused himself slipping his fingers through the empty sockets, covering the cranium with his hand to form a cap, or burying his fist in the lower cavity until he held the skull supported from the inside: then, sticking one knuckle through the triangle and another through the mouth like a long, sharp tongue, he worked his hand in a series of gestures and amused himself immensely, imagining that the thing was alive.

Not revealing his discovery to anyone, he kept it hidden for two days in the bureau, carefully wrapped, swelling the briefcase. The afternoon following his discovery, he stayed in his room, pacing nervously in the midst of his ancestors' opulent and luxurious furniture. He seldom lifted his head: it might be said that he was examining with profound devotion and some terror the bloody and magical figures in the middle circle of the carpet, but he did not even see them. At first he was undecided, worried: family complications could occur; perhaps they would laugh at him. This idea irritated him and he felt distressed and wanted to cry. From that moment on, the project never went out of his head but once: that was when, standing in front of the window, he imagined the dark pigeon house, full of holes, and remembered how at one time that little wooden house with innumerable entrances had not been empty, lifeless, but was inhabited by gray and white birds that insistently scarred the wood with their pecking and sometimes fluttered above the trees and the flowers of the gardens. He thought nostalgically about how weak and affectionate they were: trustingly, they would come and perch in his palm, where he always carried some seed for them, and when he squeezed them they would half close their eyes and a very brief tremor would shake them. Afterwards he stopped thinking about it. When the butler came to tell him that dinner was served, he had already made up his mind. That night he slept well. The next morning he forgot how he had dreamed about an evil column of large red ants that suddenly invaded the pigeon house and made the birds uneasy, while he watched the scene through a telescope from his window.

He had imagined that cleaning the skull would be somewhat difficult and quick, but he was wrong. The dust—what he had thought was dust and was, to judge from its biting odor, perhaps excrement—remained soldered to the inside walls and shone like sheet metal at the back of the cranium. While the white silk of the scarf became covered with gray stains without the coating of filth disappearing, Don Eulogio's excitement increased. At one moment, irritated, he flung the skull away, but before it stopped rolling he had repented and was out of his seat, crawling on the floor until he reached it and lifted it up carefully. Then he guessed that the cleaning might be possible if he used something greasy. Over the house phone he ordered a can of olive oil from the kitchen and waited in the doorway for the waiter, out of whose hand he tore the can violently without paying any attention to the troubled look the boy tried to throw around the room, staring over the man's shoulder. Full of anxiety, he soaked the scarf in the olive oil and, gently at first, then increasing the rhythm, he scraped to the point of exasperation. Soon he enthusiastically confirmed that the remedy worked: a soft rain of dust fell to his feet and he did not even notice that the olive oil was also dampening the edge of his cuffs and the sleeves of his jacket. Leaping to his feet suddenly, he stared in wonder at the skull he held up over his head: clean, radiant, motionless, with several little drops like sweat on the rolling surface of the cheekbones. Lovingly, he wrapped it up once again; he shut the briefcase and left the National Club. The taxi he got at Plaza San Martin dropped him off behind his house, on Orrantia. Night had fallen. In the cold semidarkness of the street he paused for a moment, fearing that the door might be locked. Weakly he stretched out his arm, and he gave a jump for joy when he realized that the handle was turning and the door was giving way with a tiny squeak.

At that moment he heard voices in the pergola. He was so wrapped up in his own thoughts that he had even forgotten the reason for his feverish activity. The voices and the movement were so unforeseen that his heart seemed like an oxygen tank connected to a dying man. His first impulse was to crouch down, but he did it so clumsily that he slipped off the rock and slid flat on his face. He felt a sharp pain in his forehead and a disagreeable taste of wet earth in his mouth, but he made no effort to stand up and stayed there, half buried in the grass, breathing laboriously, trembling. In his fall, he had had time to raise the hand that held the skull, so it had remained up in the air, a few inches from the ground, still clean.

The pergola was some fifty yards from his hiding place, and Don Eulogio heard the voices as a delicate murmuring without making out what they were saying. He got up painfully. Spying, he then saw in the middle of the arc of large apple trees, whose roots reached to the foundation of the dining room, a precise, slender silhouette, and he realized that it was his son. Next to him was a woman, still sharper and smaller, reclining with a certain abandon. It was his son's wife. Blinking, rubbing his eyes, he tried anxiously but in vain to catch a glimpse of the boy. Then he heard him laugh: a boy's crystalline laugh, spontaneous and open, that crossed the garden like a bird. He did not wait any longer; he took the candle out of his jacket and gropingly collected branches, clods of earth and pebbles, working quickly to fix the candle securely on the rock and to place the rock like an obstacle in the middle of the path. Then, with extreme precision to keep the candle balanced, he placed the skull over it. Seized with great excitement, putting his eyelashes up to the solid, oily object, he felt happy: the height was right, the candle's small white point stuck out through the hole in the cranium like a spikenard. He could not stay watching. The father had raised his voice and although his words were still incomprehensible, the old man knew they were addressed to the boy. There was something of an exchange of words among the three people: the father's heavy voice, increasingly vigorous, the melodious sound of the woman, his grandson's shrill yelps. Suddenly the noise stopped. The silence was very brief; his grandson exploded it, shrieking: "But remember—my punishment ends today. You said seven days and it's over today. Tomorrow I'm not going." With the last words he heard hurried footsteps.

Was he coming running? It was the decisive moment. Don Eulogio overcame the anguish strangling him and carried out his plan. The first match gave off only a brief blue thread. The second took fire. Burning his nails, but not feeling any pain, he kept it next to the skull, even seconds after the candle was lit. He hesitated because what he saw was not exactly what he had imagined, but then a sudden flame shot up between his hands with an abrupt crackling, like a heavy footstep in a pile of dead leaves, and the skull was completely illuminated, throwing out light from the eye sockets, the cranium, the nose and mouth. "It's all lit

up," he exclaimed in wonder. He stood still and repeated
like a record: "It was the olive oil, it was the olive oil,"
stupefied, bewitched before the fascinating skull enveloped
in flames.

Exactly at that instant he heard the shout. A savage
shout, the howl of an animal pierced by many javelins. The
boy was in front of him, his hands extended, his fingers
convulsed. Livid, shaking, his eyes and mouth open, he was
mute now and stiff, but his throat was making strange
sounds independently, snorting. "He's seen me, he's seen
me," Don Eulogio said to himself in panic. But looking at
him, he knew immediately that the boy had not seen him,
that his grandson could not see anything but that flaming
head. His eyes were fixed, with a deep, everlasting terror
painted in them. Everything had been simultaneous: the
sudden blaze, the howl, the vision of that figure in short
pants suddenly possessed by terror. Enthusiastically he was
thinking that things had turned out even more perfectly
than he had planned, when he heard approaching voices
and footsteps; and then, not caring about the noise, he
turned, and jumping off the path, trampling the beds of
chrysanthemums and roses, which he glimpsed as the re-
flection of the flame reached them, he crossed the space
separating him from the door. He ran through, accom-
panied by the woman's scream, also strident but less genu-
ine than his grandson's. He did not stop; he did not look
back. Out on the street, a cold wind cut through his forehead and his few hairs, but he did not notice it and continued walking, slowly, rubbing the garden wall with his
shoulder, smiling in satisfaction, breathing better, more
calmly.

A Visitor

The sands lap the front of the inn and come to an end there: from the hole serving as a door or from among the reeds, the view slides over a white, languid surface until it meets the sky. Behind the inn, the land is hard and rugged, and less than a mile away begin the burnished, closely ranged hills, each taller than the preceding one, their peaks piercing the clouds like needles or axes. To the left, the narrow, winding wood stretches along the border of the sand and grows without a break until it disappears between two hills, far beyond the inn: underbrush, wild plants and a dry, rampant grass that hides everything—the uneven terrain, the snakes, the tiny swamps. But the wood is only a hint of the forest, a foretaste: it stops at the end of a ravine, at the foot of a massive hill beyond which the real forest begins. And Doña Merceditas knows it: once, years ago, she climbed to the top of that mountain and with astonished eyes gazed through the large patches of cloud floating beneath her feet at the green platform stretching far and wide without a clearing.

Now Doña Merceditas dozes, lying across two sacks. A

little farther away, the goat pokes his nose in the sand, stubbornly chews a splinter of wood or bleats in the cool afternoon air. Suddenly, it pricks up its ears and freezes. The woman half opens her eyes.

"What's up, Cuera?"

The animal pulls on the cord tying it to the stake. The woman laboriously stands up. Some fifty yards away, the man is silhouetted sharply against the horizon, his shadow preceding him across the sand. The woman shades her forehead with one hand. She looks around quickly; then she stands motionless. The man is very close; he is tall, emaciated, quite dark, with curly hair and mocking eyes. His faded shirt flutters outside his flannel pants, which are rolled up to his knees. His legs look like two black pegs.

"Good afternoon, Doña Merceditas." His voice is melodious and sarcastic. The woman has turned pale.

"What do you want?" she murmurs.

"You recognize me, right? Well, good for you. If you'd be so kind, I'd like something to eat. And drink. I'm really thirsty."

"There's beer and fruit inside."

"Thanks, Señora Merceditas. You're very kind. Like always. Will you join me?"

"What for?" The woman looks at him distrustfully. She is fat and well along in years, but with smooth skin. She is barefoot. "You know the place already."

"Oh!" the man says in a cordial way. "I don't like to eat alone. Makes me sad."

The woman hesitates for a moment. Then she walks toward the inn, dragging her feet in the sand. She goes in. She opens a bottle of beer.

"Thanks, thanks a lot, Señora Merceditas. But I prefer

milk. Since you've opened that bottle, why don't you drink it?"

"I don't feel like it."

"C'mon, Señora Merceditas, don't be like that. Drink to my health."

"I don't want to."

The man's face goes sour. "Are you deaf? I told you to drink that bottle. Cheers!"

The woman raises the bottle with both hands and drinks slowly in small sips. On the dirty, scratched counter a bottle of milk glitters. With a swipe of his hand, the man scares off the flies circling around it, raises the bottle and takes a long drink. His lips are covered with a muzzle of cream, which his tongue, seconds later, noisily wipes away.

"Ah!" he says, licking again. "That milk really was good, Señora Merceditas. Goat's milk, isn't it? I liked it a lot. Have you finished that bottle yet? Why don't you open up another? Cheers!"

The woman obeys without protest; the man devours two bananas and an orange.

"Listen, Señora Merceditas, don't go so fast. The beer's running down your neck. It's going to get your dress wet. Don't waste things that way. Open up another bottle and drink to Numa. Cheers!"

The man goes on repeating "Cheers!" until there are four empty bottles on the counter. The woman's eyes are glassy; she belches, spits, sits down on a sack of fruit.

"My God!" says the man. "Some woman! You're a regular drunk, Señora Merceditas. Excuse me for telling you so."

"You're going to be sorry for what you're doing to a poor old lady. You'll see, Jamaican, you'll see." Her tongue is a little thick.

"Really?" the man says, bored. "By the way, what time's Numa coming?"

"Numa?"

"Oh, you're really awful, Señora Merceditas, when you don't want to understand something. What time's he coming?"

"You're a filthy nigger, Jamaican. Numa's going to kill you."

"Don't talk that way, Señora Merceditas!" He yawns. "All right, I think we've still got a while yet. Definitely until nighttime. We're going to take a little nap, that okay with you?"

He gets up and goes out. He heads toward the goat. The animal looks at him suspiciously. He unties it. He goes back to the inn, swinging the cord like a propeller and whistling; the woman is gone. The lazy, lewd calmness of his gestures disappears immediately. Swearing, he runs around the place in great leaps. Then he heads toward the wood, followed by the goat. The animal finds the woman behind a tree and begins to lick her. The Jamaican laughs, seeing the angry looks the woman flings at the goat. He makes a simple gesture and Doña Merceditas heads toward the inn.

"You really are an awful woman, yessiree. What notions you've got!"

He ties her feet and hands. Then he picks her up easily and deposits her on the counter. He stands there looking at her wickedly and, suddenly, starts tickling the broad, wrinkled soles of her feet. The woman writhes with laughter; her face shows her desperation. The counter is narrow and with her shaking Doña Merceditas nears the edge; finally, she rolls heavily onto the floor.

"What an awful woman, yessiree!" he repeats. "You pretend to faint and you're spying on me out of one eye. There's no curing you, Señora Merceditas!"

Its head thrust into the room, the goat stares at the woman attentively.

The neighing of the horses cuts through the end of the afternoon: it is already growing dark. Señora Merceditas raises her head and listens, her eyes wide open.

"It's them," says the Jamaican. He jumps up. The horses keep neighing and pawing. From the door of the inn, the man shouts angrily:

"You gone nuts, Lieutenant? You gone nuts?"

Out of a rocky bend in the hill the lieutenant appears: he is short and thick-set; he is wearing riding boots and his face is sweaty. He looks around warily.

"You nuts?" repeats the Jamaican. "What's the matter with you?"

"Don't raise your voice at me, nigger," says the lieutenant. "We just got here. What's going on?"

"What do you mean, what's going on? Order your men to take their horses away. Don't you know your job?"

The lieutenant turns red.

"You're not free yet, nigger," he says. "Show some respect."

"Hide the horses and cut their tongues out if you like. Just so they're not heard. And wait there. I'll give you the signal." The Jamaican uncurls his mouth and the smile sketched on his face is insolent. "Don't you see that now you've got to follow my orders?"

The lieutenant hesitates for a few seconds.

"God help you if he doesn't come," he says. And, turning his head, he orders: "Sergeant Lituma, hide the horses."

"Yes, sir, Lieutenant," says someone from behind the

hill. The sound of hoofs is heard. Then silence.

"Good for you," says the Jamaican. "You got to follow orders. Very good, General. Bravo, Commander. Congratulations, Captain. Don't move from that spot. I'll let you know."

The lieutenant shows him his fist and disappears among the rocks. The Jamaican goes into the inn. The woman's eyes are filled with hatred.

"Double-crosser," she mumbles. "You've come with the police. Damn you!"

"What manners, my God, what bad manners you've got, Señora Merceditas! I didn't come with the police. I came alone. I met the lieutenant here. That should be obvious to you."

"Numa's not coming," says the woman. "And the police will cart you off to jail again. And when you get out, Numa will kill you."

"You've got hard feelings, Señora Merceditas, no doubt about it. The things you predict for me!"

"Double-crosser," repeats the woman; she has managed to sit up and stays very stiff. "Do you think Numa's stupid?"

"Stupid? Not at all. He's a real fox. But don't give up, Señora Merceditas. I'm sure he'll come."

"He isn't coming. He's not like you—he's got friends. They'll warn him the police are here."

"Think so? I don't. They won't have time. The police have come from around the other side, from behind the hills. I crossed the sand alone. In every town I asked, 'Is Señora Merceditas still at the inn? They just let me out and I'm going to wring her neck.' At least twenty people must've run to tell Numa. Still think he won't come? My God, what a face you've put on, Señora Merceditas!"

"If anything happens to Numa," stammers the woman

hoarsely, "you're going to regret it for the rest of your life, Jamaican."

He shrugs. He lights up a cigarette and begins to whistle. Then he goes up to the counter, takes the oil lamp and lights it. He hangs it on the door.

"It's getting dark," he says. "Come over here, Señora Merceditas. I want Numa to see you sitting in the doorway, waiting for him. Oh! That's right. You can't move. Excuse me, I'm so forgetful."

He bends over and lifts her in his arms. He puts her down in the sand in front of the inn. The light from the lamp falls on the woman and softens the skin on her face: she looks younger.

"Why are you doing this, Jamaican?" By now the voice of Doña Merceditas is weak.

"Why?" asks the Jamaican. "You haven't been in jail, have you, Señora Merceditas? Day after day goes by and you haven't got anything to do. Let me tell you, you really get bored in there. And you're hungry a lot. Listen, I forgot about one detail. You can't have your mouth hanging open. You can't start shouting when Numa comes. Besides, you might swallow a fly."

He laughs. He looks around the room and finds a rag. With it he bandages half of Doña Merceditas's face. Amused, he examines her for a long while.

"Let me tell you, you look really funny that way, Señora Merceditas. I just don't know what you look like."

In the darkness at the back of the inn, the Jamaican rises up like a serpent: elastically and noiselessly. He remains bent over, his hands resting on the counter. Two yards in front of him in the circle of light the woman is rigid, her face pushed forward as if she were sniffing the air: she too has heard. It was a slight but very distinct sound, coming from the left, standing out above the crickets' singing. It bursts out again, longer: the branches in the wood crackle and break. Something is approaching the inn. "He's not alone," whispers the Jamaican. "There're several of them." He reaches into his pocket, pulls out the whistle and places it between his lips. He waits, not moving. The woman stirs and the Jamaican curses between his teeth. He sees her squirm in place and jerk her head left and right, trying to free herself from the gag. The noise has stopped: is he already on the sand, which muffles his footsteps? The woman has her face turned toward the left and her eyes, like a squashed iguana's, bulge from their sockets. "She's seen them," the Jamaican mutters. He places the tip of his tongue on the whistle: the metal is sharp. Doña Merceditas goes on twisting her head and groans in anguish. The goat bleats and the Jamaican crouches down. Seconds later he sees a shadow descending over the woman and a naked arm stretching toward the gag. He blows with all his might at the same time that he jumps on the newcomer. The whistle fills the night like a fire and is lost amid the curses exploding right and left, followed by hurried footsteps. The two men have fallen on the woman. The lieutenant is fast: when the Jamaican stands up, one of his hands seizes Numa by the hair and the other holds the revolver to his temple. Four guards with rifles surround them.

"Run!" shouts the Jamaican to the guards. "The others are in the wood. Quick! They're going to get away. Quick!"

"Keep still!" shouts the lieutenant. He does not take his eyes off Numa, who is trying, out of the corner of his eye, to find the revolver. He seems calm; his hands hang at his sides.

"Sergeant Lituma, tie him up."

Lituma puts his rifle on the ground and uncoils the rope he has at his waist. He ties Numa by his feet and then handcuffs him. The goat has come up and, smelling Numa's legs, begins to lick them gently.

"The horses, Sergeant Lituma."

The lieutenant sticks the revolver back in his holster and bends toward the woman. He takes off the gag and the ropes. Doña Merceditas stands up and goes to Numa after kicking the goat out of the way. She strokes his forehead without saying anything.

"What's he done to you?" asks Numa.

"Nothing," says the woman. "Want a cigarette?"

"Lieutenant," insists the Jamaican. "Do you realize the others are there in the woods, just a few yards away? Didn't you hear them? There must be at least three or four. What're you waiting for? To order a search for them?"

"Shut up, nigger," says the lieutenant, without looking at him. He strikes a match and lights the cigarette the woman has put in Numa's mouth. Numa begins to suck in long puffs; the cigarette is between his teeth and he blows the smoke out through his nose. "I came looking for this guy. Nobody else."

"Okay," says the Jamaican. "So much the worse if you don't know your job. I did mine. I'm free."

"Yeah," says the lieutenant. "You're free."

"The horses, Lieutenant," says Lituma. He holds the reins of five animals.

"Put him up on your horse, Lituma," says the lieutenant. "He'll go with you."

The sergeant and another guard take Numa and, after untying his feet, seat him on the horse. Lituma mounts behind him. The lieutenant moves toward the horses and takes up the reins of his own.

"Listen, Lieutenant, who'm I going with?"

"You?" says the lieutenant, with one foot in the stirrup. "You?"

"Yeah," says the Jamaican. "Who else?"

"You're free," says the lieutenant. "You don't have to come with us. You can go wherever you like."

From their horses, Lituma and the other guards laugh.

"What kind of joke is this?" asks the Jamaican. His voice is trembling. "You're not going to leave me here, are you, Lieutenant? You can hear the noises in the woods. I've behaved myself. I did my part. You can't do this to me."

"If we ride fast, Sergeant Lituma," says the lieutenant, "we'll reach Piura by dawn. It's better to travel through the desert at night. The animals don't get so tired."

"Lieutenant," shouts the Jamaican. He has grabbed the reins of the officer's horse and shakes them frantically. "You can't leave me here. You can't do such a spiteful thing!"

The lieutenant lifts one foot out of the stirrup and kicks the Jamaican away, hard.

"We'll have to gallop from time to time," says the lieutenant. "Think it'll rain, Sergeant Lituma?"

"I don't think so, Lieutenant. Sky's clear."

"You can't leave without me!" the Jamaican hollers at the top of his voice.

Señora Merceditas begins to laugh loudly, holding her stomach.

"Let's get moving," says the lieutenant.

"Lieutenant!" shouts the Jamaican. "Please, Lieutenant, please!"

Slowly the horses go off. The Jamaican watches them, dazed. The light from the lamp shines on his contorted face. Señora Merceditas continues to laugh thunderously.

Suddenly she grows quiet. She cups her hands around her mouth.

"Numa!" she shouts. "I'll bring you fruit on Sundays."

Then she starts laughing again at the top of her lungs. Out of the wood comes the sound of snapping branches and dry leaves.

On Sunday

He held his breath for an instant, dug his fingernails into the palms of his hands and said very quickly: "I'm in love with you." He saw her blush suddenly, as if someone had slapped her cheeks, which were radiantly pale and very smooth. Terrified, he felt his confusion rising in him, petrifying his tongue. He wanted to run away, to put an end to it: in the gloomy winter morning there rose up from deep inside him the weakness that always discouraged him at decisive moments. A few minutes before, in the midst of the lively, smiling crowd strolling in Miraflores' Central Park, Miguel was still repeating to himself: "Right now. When we get to Pardo Avenue. I'll get up the nerve. Oh, Rubén, if you knew how much I hate you!" And still earlier at church, seeking out Flora, he had glimpsed her at the base of a column and, opening a path with his elbows without begging pardon of the women he was pushing aside, succeeded in getting close to her. Saying hello in a low voice, he repeated to himself, stubbornly, as he had that dawn lying in his bed, watching day break: "There's no other way. I've got to do it today. In the morning. You'll pay for this yet, Rubén." And the

night before, he had cried for the first time in many years
when he realized how that dirty trick was being planned.
People were staying in the park and Pardo Avenue was
deserted. They walked down the tree-lined promenade
under the tall, densely crowned rubber trees. I've got to
get a move on, Miguel thought, if I'm not going to foul
myself up. Out of the corner of his eye he looked around
him: there was no one about; he could try. Slowly, he
stretched out his left hand until it touched hers; the contact made him aware that he was sweating. He begged for
some miracle to happen, for that humiliation to be over.
What do I say to her now? he thought. What do I say to
her now? She had pulled back her hand and he was feeling forsaken and silly. All his brilliant lines, feverishly re-
hearsed the night before, had dissolved like soap bubbles.

"Flora," he stammered, "I've waited a long time for this
moment. Ever since I met you, you're all I think about. I'm
in love for the first time, believe me. I've never known a girl
like you."

Once again a compacted white space in his brain—a void.
The pressure could not get any higher: his skin gave way
like rubber and his fingernails struck bone. Still, he went on
talking with difficulty, pausing, overcoming his embarrassed stammer, trying to describe an impulsive, consum-
ing passion until he found with relief that they had reached
the first circle on Pardo Avenue, and then he fell silent.
Flora lived between the second and third trees past the
oval. They stopped and looked at each other: Flora was still
red, and being flustered had filled her eyes with a moist
brightness. Despairing, Miguel told himself that she had
never looked more beautiful: a blue ribbon held her hair
back and he could see the start of her neck as well as her
ears, two tiny, perfect question marks.

"Look, Miguel," Flora said; her voice was gentle, full of music, steady. "I can't answer you right now. But my mother doesn't want me to go with boys till I finish school."

"Flora, all mothers say the same thing," Miguel insisted. "How's she going to find out? We'll see each other whenever you say, even if it's only on Sundays."

"I'll give you an answer but first I've got to think it over," Flora said, lowering her eyes. And after several seconds she added: "Excuse me, but I have to go now; it's getting late."

Miguel felt a deep weariness, a feeling that spread throughout his entire body and relaxed him.

"You're not mad at me, Flora?" he asked humbly.

"Don't be silly," she replied animatedly. "I'm not mad."

"I'll wait as long as you want," Miguel said. "But we'll keep on seeing each other, won't we? We'll go to the movies this afternoon, okay?"

"I can't this afternoon," she said softly. "Martha's asked me over to her house."

A hot, violent flush ran through him and he felt wounded, stunned at this answer, which he had been expecting and which now seemed cruel to him. What Melanés had insidiously whispered into his ear Saturday afternoon was right. Martha would leave them alone; it was the usual trick. Later Rubén would tell the gang how he and his sister had planned the situation, the place and the time. As payment for her services, Martha would have demanded the right to spy from behind the curtain. Anger suddenly drenched his hands.

"Don't be like that, Flora. Let's go to the matinee like we said. I won't talk to you about this. I promise."

"I can't, really," Flora said. "I've got to go to Martha's. She stopped by my house to ask me yesterday. But later I'll go to Salazar Park with her."

He did not see any hope even in those last words. A little later he was gazing at the spot where the frail, angelic figure had disappeared under the majestic arch of the rubber trees along the avenue. It was possible to compete with a mere adversary, not with Rubén. He recalled the names of girls invited by Martha, other Sunday afternoons. Now he was unable to do anything; he was defeated. Then, once more, there came to mind that image which saved him every time he experienced frustration: out of a distant background of clouds puffed up with black smoke, at the head of a company of cadets from the naval academy, he approached a reviewing stand set up in the park; illustrious men in formal attire with top hats in hand, and ladies with glittering jewels were applauding him. A crowd, in which the faces of his friends and enemies stood out, packed the sidewalks and watched him in wonder, whispering his name. Dressed in blue, a full cape flowing from his shoulders, Miguel led the march, looking toward the horizon. His sword was raised, his head described a half circle in the air; there at the center of the reviewing stand was Flora, smiling. He saw Rubén off in one corner, in tatters and ashamed, and confined himself to a brief, disdainful glance as he marched on, disappearing amid hurrahs.

Like steam wiped off a mirror, the image vanished. He was at the door of his house; he hated everyone, he hated himself. He entered and went straight up to his room, throwing himself face down on the bed. In the cool darkness, the girl's face appeared between his eyes and their lids —"I love you, Flora," he said out loud—and then Rubén with his insolent jaw and hostile smile: the faces were alongside each other; they came closer. Rubén's eyes twisted in order to look at him mockingly while his mouth approached Flora.

He jumped up from the bed. The closet mirror showed him an ashen face with dark circles under the eyes. "He won't see her," he decided. "He won't do this to me; I won't let him play that dirty trick on me."

Pardo Avenue was still deserted. Stepping up his pace without pausing, he walked to the intersection at Grau Avenue. He hesitated there. He felt cold: he had left his jacket in his room and just his shirt was not enough to protect him from the wind blowing off the sea and tangling itself with a soft murmuring in the dense branches of the rubber trees. The dreaded image of Flora and Rubén together gave him courage and he continued walking. From the doorway of the bar next to the Montecarlo movie house, he saw them at their usual table, lords of the corner formed by the rear and left-hand walls. Francisco, Melanés, Tobias, the Brain —they all noticed him and after a moment's surprise turned toward Rubén, their faces wicked and excited. He recovered his poise immediately: in front of men he certainly did know how to behave.

"Hello!" he said to them, drawing near. "What's new?"

"Sit down," said the Brain, pushing a chair toward him. "What miracle's brought you here?"

"You haven't been around here for ages," Francisco said.

"I felt like seeing you," Miguel answered pleasantly. "I knew you'd be here. What's so surprising? Or aren't I one of the Hawks anymore?"

He took a seat between Melanés and Tobias. Rubén was across from him.

"Cuncho!" shouted the Brain. "Bring another glass. One that's not too greasy."

Cuncho brought the glass and the Brain filled it with beer. Miguel said, "To the Hawks," and drank.

"You might as well drink the glass while you're at it," Francisco said. "You sure are thirsty!"

"I bet you went to one o'clock mass," said Melanés, winking in satisfaction as he always did when he was starting some mischief. "Right?"

"I did," Miguel said, unruffled. "But just to see a chick, nothing else."

He looked at Rubén with defiant eyes but Rubén did not let on; he was drumming his fingers on the table and whistling very softly, with the point of his tongue between his teeth, Pérez Prado's "The Popoff Girl."

"Great!" applauded Melanés. "Okay, Don Juan. Tell us, which chick?"

"That's a secret."

"There are no secrets between Hawks," Tobias reminded him. "You forget already? C'mon, who was it?"

"What's it to you?" Miguel asked.

"A lot," Tobias said. "Got to know who you're going around with to know who you are."

"You lost that round," Melanés said to Miguel. "One to nothing."

"I'll bet I can guess who it is," Francisco said. "You guys don't know?"

"I do already," Tobias said.

"Me too," said Melanés. He turned to Rubén with very innocent eyes and voice. "And you, brother, can you guess who it is?"

"No," said Rubén coldly. "And I don't care."

"My stomach's on fire," said the Brain. "Nobody's going to get a beer?"

Melanés drew a pathetic finger across his throat. "I have not money, darling," he said in English.

"I'll buy a bottle," announced Tobias with a solemn gesture. "Let's see who follows my example. We've got to put out the fire in this booby."

"Cuncho, bring half a dozen bottles of Cristal," said Miguel.

There were shouts of joy, exclamations.

"You're a real Hawk," Francisco declared.

"A friendly son of a bitch, " added Melanés. "Yeah, a real super Hawk."

Cuncho brought the beers. They drank. They listened to Melanés telling dirty, crude, wild, hot stories and Tobias and Francisco started up a heavy discussion about soccer. The Brain told an anecdote. He was on his way from Lima to Miraflores by bus. The other passengers got off at Arequipa Avenue. At the top of Javier Prado, Tomasso, the White Whale, got on—that albino who's six feet four and still in grammar school, lives in Quebrada, you with me? Pretending to be really interested in the bus, he started asking the driver questions, leaning over the seat in front of him while he was slowly slitting the upholstery on the back of the seat with his knife.

"He was doing it because I was there," asserted the Brain. "He wanted to show off."

"He's a mental retard," said Francisco. "You do things like that when you're ten. They're not funny at his age."

"What happened afterwards is funny." The Brain laughed. " 'Listen, driver, can't you see that whale's destroying your bus?' "

"What?" yelled the driver, screeching to a stop. His ears burning, his eyes popping out, Tomasso the White Whale was forcing the door open.

"With his knife," the Brain said. "Look how he's left the seat."

At last the White Whale managed to get out. He started running down Arequipa Avenue. The driver ran after him, shouting, "Catch that bastard!"

"Did he catch him?" Melanés asked.

"Don't know. I beat it. And I stole the ignition key as a souvenir. Here it is."

He took a small, silver-plated key out of his pocket and tossed it onto the table. The bottles were empty. Rubén looked at his watch and stood up.

"I'm going," he said. "See you later."

"Don't go," said Miguel. "I'm rich today. I'll buy us all lunch."

A flurry of slaps landed on his back; the Hawks thanked him loudly, they sang his praises.

"I can't," Rubén said. "I've got things to do."

"Go on, get going, boy," Tobias said. "And give Martha my regards."

"We'll be thinking of you all the time, brother," Melanés said.

"No," Miguel yelled out. "I'm inviting everybody or nobody. If Rubén goes, that's it."

"Now you've heard it, Hawk Rubén," Francisco said. "You've got to stay."

"You've got to stay," Melanés said. "No two ways about it."

"I'm going," Rubén said.

"Trouble is, you're drunk," said Miguel. "You're going because you're scared of looking silly in front of us, that's the trouble."

"How many times have I carried you home dead drunk?" asked Rubén. "How many times have I helped you up the railing so your father wouldn't catch you? I can hold ten times as much as you."

"You used to," Miguel said. "Now it's rough. Want to see?"

"With pleasure," Rubén answered. "We'll meet tonight, right here?"

"No, right now." Miguel turned toward the others, spreading his arms wide. "Hawks, I'm making a challenge."

Delighted, he proved that the old formula still had the same force as before. In the midst of the happy commotion he had stirred up, he saw Rubén sit down, pale.

"Cuncho!" Tobias shouted. "The menu. And two swimming pools of beer. A Hawk has just made a challenge."

They ordered steak with spiced onions and a dozen beers. Tobias lined up three bottles for each of the competitors and the rest for the others. They ate, scarcely speaking. Miguel took a drink after each mouthful and tried to look lively, but his fear of not being able to hold enough beer mounted in proportion to the sour taste at the back of his throat. They finished off the six bottles long after Cuncho had removed the plates.

"You order," Miguel said to Rubén.

"Three more each."

After the first glass of the new round, Miguel heard a buzzing in his ears; his head was a slow-spinning roulette wheel and everything was whirling.

"I've got to take a piss," he said. "I'm going to the bathroom."

The Hawks laughed.

"Give up?" Rubén asked.

"I'm going to take a piss," Miguel shouted. "If you want to, order more."

In the bathroom he vomited. Then he washed his face over and over, trying to erase all the telltale signs. His watch said four-thirty. Despite his heavy sickness, he felt happy. Now Rubén was powerless. He went back to their table.

"Cheers," Rubén said, raising his glass.

He's furious, Miguel thought. But I've fixed him now.

"Smells like a dead body," Melanés said. "Somebody's dying on us around here."

"I'm fresh as a daisy," Miguel asserted, trying to hold back his dizziness and nausea.

"Cheers," Rubén repeated.

When they had finished the last beer, his stomach felt like lead; the voices of the others reached his ears as a confused mixture of sounds. A hand suddenly appeared under his eyes; it was white with long fingers; it caught him by the chin; it forced him to raise his head; Rubén's face had gotten larger. He was funny-looking, so rumpled and mad.

"Give up, snot-nose?"

Miguel stood up suddenly and shoved Rubén, but before the show could go on, the Brain stepped in.

"Hawks never fight," he said, forcing them to sit down. "You two are drunk. It's over. Let's vote."

Against their will, Melanés, Francisco and Tobias agreed to a tie.

"I'd won already," Rubén said. "This one can't even talk. Look at him."

As a matter of fact, Miguel's eyes were glassy, his mouth hung open and a thread of saliva dribbled off his tongue.

"Shut up," said the Brain. "We wouldn't call you any champion at beer drinking."

"You're no beer-drinking champion," Melanés emphasized. "You're just a champion at swimming, the wizard of the pools."

"You better shut up," Rubén said. "Can't you see your envy's eating you alive?"

"Long live the Esther Williams of Miraflores!" shouted Melanés.

"An old codger like you and you don't even know how to swim," said Rubén. "You want me to give you some lessons?"

"We know already, champ," the Brain said. "You won a swimming championship. And all the chicks are dying over you. You're a regular little champion."

"He's no champion of anything," Miguel said with difficulty. "He's just a phony."

"You're keeling over," Rubén answered. "Want me to take you home, girlie?"

"I'm not drunk," Miguel protested. "And you're just a phony."

"You're pissed because I'm going to go steady with Flora," Rubén said. "You're dying of jealousy. Think I don't understand things?"

"Just a phony," Miguel said. "You won because your father's union president; everybody knows he pulled a fast one, and you only won on account of that."

"At least I swim better than you," Rubén said. "You don't even know how to surf."

"You don't swim better than anybody," Miguel said. "Any girl can leave you behind."

"Any girl," said Melanés. "Even Miguel, who's a mother."

"Pardon me while I laugh," Rubén said.

"You're pardoned, your Highness," Tobias said.

"You're getting at me because it's winter," Rubén said. "If it wasn't, I'd challenge you all to go to the beach to see who's so cocksure in the water."

"You won the championship on account of your father,"

Miguel said. "You're just a phony. When you want to swim with me, just let me know—don't be so timid. At the beach, at Terraces, wherever you want."

"At the beach," Rubén said. "Right now."

"You're just a phony," Miguel said.

Rubén's face suddenly lit up and in addition to being spiteful, his eyes became arrogant again.

"I'll bet you on who's in the water first," he said.

"Just a phony," said Miguel.

"If you win," Rubén said, "I promise you I'll lay off Flora. And if I win, you can go peddle your wares someplace else."

"Who do you think you are?" Miguel stammered. "Asshole, just who do you think you are?"

"Listen, Hawks," Rubén said, spreading his arms, "I'm making a challenge."

"Miguel's in no shape now," the Brain said. "Why don't you two flip a coin for Flora?"

"And why're you butting in?" Miguel said. "I accept. Let's go to the beach."

"You're both crazy," Francisco said. "I'm not going down to the beach in this cold. Make another bet."

"He's accepted," Rubén said. "Let's go."

"When a Hawk challenges somebody, we all bite our tongues," Melanés said. "Let's go to the beach. And if they don't have the guts to go into the water, we throw them in."

"Those two are smashed," insisted the Brain. "The challenge doesn't hold."

"Shut up, Brain," Miguel roared. "I'm a big boy now. I don't need you to take care of me."

"Okay," said the Brain, shrugging his shoulders. "Screw you, then."

They left. Outside, a quiet gray atmosphere was waiting

for them. Miguel breathed in deeply; he felt better. Francisco, Melanés and Rubén walked in front; behind them, Miguel and the Brain. There were pedestrians on Grau Avenue, mostly maids on their day off in gaudy dresses. Ashen men with thick, lanky hair preyed around them and looked them over greedily. The women laughed, showing their gold teeth. The Hawks did not pay any attention to them. They walked on with long strides as the excitement mounted in them.

"Better now?" asked the Brain.

"Yeah," answered Miguel. "The air's done me good."

They turned the corner at Pardo Avenue. They marched in a line, spread out like a squadron under the rubber trees of the promenade, over the flagstones heaved up at intervals by the enormous roots that sometimes pushed through the surface like grappling hooks. Going down the crosstown street, they passed two girls. Rubén bowed ceremoniously.

"Hi, Rubén," they sang in duet.

Tobias imitated them in falsetto: "Hi, Rubén, you prince."

The crosstown street ends at a forking brook: on one side winds the embankment, paved and shiny; on the other a slope that goes around the hill and reaches the sea. It is known as the "bathhouse path"; its pavement is worn smooth and shiny from automobile tires and the feet of swimmers from many, many summers.

"Let's warm up, champs," Melanés shouted, breaking into a sprint. The others followed his example.

They ran against the wind and light fog rising off the beach, caught up in an exciting whirlwind: through their ears, mouths and noses the air penetrated to their lungs and a sensation of relief and well-being spread through their bodies as the drop became steeper, and at one point their feet no longer obeyed anything but a mysterious force coming from the depths of the earth. Their arms like propellers, a salty taste on their tongues, the Hawks descended the slope at a full run until they reached the circular platform suspended over the bathhouse. Some fifty yards offshore, the sea vanished in a thick cloud that seemed about to charge the cliffs, those high, dark breakwaters jutting up around the entire bay.

"Let's go back," said Francisco. "I'm cold."

At the edge of the platform is a railing, stained in places by moss. An opening marks the top of the nearly vertical stairway leading down to the beach. From up there the Hawks looked down on a short ribbon of open water at their feet and the strange, bubbling surface where the fog was blending with the foam off the waves.

"I'll go back if this guy gives up," Rubén said.

"Who's talking about giving up?" responded Miguel. "Who the hell do you think you are?"

Rubén went down the stairway three steps at a time, unbuttoning his shirt as he descended.

"Rubén!" shouted the Brain. "Are you nuts? Come back!"

But Miguel and the others were also going down and the Brain followed them.

From the balcony of the long, wide building that nestles against the hill and houses the dressing rooms, down to the curving edge of the sea, there is a slope of gray stone where people sun themselves during the summer. From morning to dusk the small beach boils with excitement. Now the water covered the slope and there were no brightly colored umbrellas or lithe girls with tanned bodies, no reverberating, melodramatic screams from children and women when a wave succeeded in splashing them before it retreated, dragging murmuring stones and round pebbles. Not even a strip of beach could be seen, since the tide came in as far as the space bounded by the dark columns holding the building up in the air. Where the undertow began, the wooden steps and cement supports, decorated by stalactites and algae, were barely visible.

"You can't see the surf," said Rubén. "How're we going to do this?"

They were in the left-hand gallery, in the women's section; their faces were serious.

"Wait till tomorrow," the Brain said. "By noon it'll be clear. Then we'll be able to check on you."

"Since we're here, let's do it now," Melanés said. "They can check on themselves."

"Okay with me," Rubén said. "And you?"

"Me too," Miguel said.

When they had stripped, Tobias joked about the blue veins scaling Miguel's smooth stomach. They went down. Licked incessantly by the water for months on end, the wooden steps were smooth and slippery. Holding on to the iron railing so as not to fall, Miguel felt a shivering mount from the soles of his feet up to his brain. He thought that in one way the fog and the cold favored him: winning now did not depend on skill so much as on endurance, and Rubén's skin was purplish too, puckered in millions of tiny goose bumps. One step below, Rubén's athletic body bent over: tense, he was waiting for the ebb of the undertow and the arrival of the next wave, which came in noiselessly, airily, casting a spray of foamy droplets before it. When the crest of the wave was six feet from the step, Rubén plunged in: with his arms out like spears and his hair on end from the momentum of his leap, his body cut straight through the air and he fell without bending, without lowering his head or tucking his legs in; he bounced in the foam, scarcely went under, and immediately taking advantage of the tide, he glided out into the water, his arms surfacing and sinking in the midst of a frantic bubbling and his feet tracing a precise, rapid wake. Miguel in turn climbed down one more step and waited for the next wave. He knew that the water was shallow there and that he should hurl himself like a plank, hard and rigid, without moving a muscle, or he would crash into the rocks. He closed his eyes and jumped and he did not hit bottom, but his body was whipped from forehead to knees and he felt a fierce stinging as he swam with all his might in order to restore to his limbs the warmth that the water had suddenly snatched from them. He was in that strange section of the sea near the shore at Miraflores where the undertow and the waves meet and there are whirlpools and crosscurrents, and the summer months were so far in the past that Miguel had forgotten how to clear it without stress. He did not recall that you had to relax your body and yield, allowing yourself to be carried along submissively in the drift, to stroke only when you rose on a wave and were at the crest in that smooth water flowing with the foam and floating on top of the currents. He did not recall that it is better to endure patiently and with some cunning that first contact with the exasperating sea along the shore that tugs at your limbs and hurls streams of water in your mouth and eyes, better to offer no resistance, to be a cork, to take in air only when a wave approaches, to go under—scarcely if they broke far out and without force or to the very bottom if the crest was nearby—to grab hold of some rock and, always on the alert, to wait out the deafening thunder of its passing, to push off in a single movement and to continue advancing, furtively, by hand strokes, until finding a new obstacle, and then going limp, not fighting the whirlpools, to swirl deliberately in the sluggish eddy and to escape suddenly, at the right moment, with a single stroke. Then a calm surface unexpectedly appears, disturbed only by harmless ripples; the water is clear, smooth, and in some spots the murky underwater rocks are visible.

After crossing the rough water, Miguel paused, exhausted, and took in air. He saw Rubén not far off, looking at him. His hair fell over his forehead in bangs; his teeth were clenched.

"Do we go on?"

"We go on."

After a few minutes of swimming, Miguel felt the cold, which had momentarily disappeared, invade him again, and he speeded up his kicking because it was in his legs, above all in his calves, that the water affected him most, numbing them first and hardening them later. He swam with his face in the water and every time his right arm came out, he turned his head to exhale the breath he had held in and to take in another supply, with which he scarcely submerged his forehead and chin once again so as not to slow his own motion and, on the contrary, to slice the water like a prow and to make his sliding through it easier. With each stroke, out of one eye he could see Rubén, swimming smoothly on the surface, effortlessly, kicking up no foam now, with the grace and ease of a gliding seagull. Miguel tried to forget Rubén and the sea and the surf (which must still be far out, since the water was clear, calm and crossed only by newly formed waves). He wanted to remember only Flora's face, the down on her arms which on sunny days glimmered like a little forest of golden threads, but he could not prevent the girl's image from being replaced by another—misty, usurping, deafening—which fell over Flora and concealed her: the image of a mountain of furious water, not exactly the surf (which he had reached once, two summers ago, and whose waves were violent with green and murky foam because at that spot, more or less, the rocks came to an end, giving rise to the mud that the waves churned to the surface and mixed with nests of algae and jellyfish, staining the sea) but rather a real ocean tormented by internal cataclysms whipping up monstrous waves that could have encompassed an entire ship and capsized it with surprising quickness, hurling into the air passengers, launches, masts, sails, buoys, sailors, portholes and flags.

He stopped swimming, his body sinking until it was vertical; he lifted his head and saw Rubén moving off. He thought of calling to him on any pretext, of saying to him, for example, "Why don't we rest for a minute?" but he did not do it. All the cold in his body seemed concentrated in his calves; he could feel his stiffened muscles, his taut skin, his accelerated heart. He moved his feet feverishly. He was at the center of a circle of dark water, walled in by the fog. He tried to catch sight of the beach or the shadow of the cliffs when the mist let up, but that vague gauze which dissolved as he cut through was not transparent. He saw only a small, greenish-black patch and a cover of clouds level with the water. Then he felt afraid. He was suddenly struck by the memory of the beer he had drunk and thought: I guess that's weakened me. In an instant it seemed as if his legs and arms had disappeared. He decided to turn back, but after a few strokes in the direction of the beach, he made an about-face and swam as gently as he could. "I won't reach the shore alone," he said to himself. "It's better to be close to Rubén; if I wear out, I'll tell him he beat me but let's go back." Now he was swimming wildly, his head up, swallowing water, flailing the sea with stiff arms, his gaze fixed on the imperturbable form ahead of him.

The movement and effort brought his legs back to life; his body regained some of its heat, the distance separating him from Ruben had decreased and that made him feel calmer. He overtook him a little later; he stretched out an arm and grabbed one of his feet. Rubén stopped instantly. His eyes were bright red and his mouth was open.

"I think we've gotten turned around," Miguel said. "Seems to me we're swimming parallel to the beach."

His teeth were chattering but his voice was steady. Rubén looked all around. Miguel watched him, tense.

"You can't see the beach anymore," Rubén said.

"You couldn't for some time," Miguel said. "There's a lot of fog."

"We're not turned around," Rubén said. "Look. Now you can see the surf."

As a matter of fact, some small waves were approaching them, with a fringe of foam that dissolved and suddenly re-formed. They looked at each other in silence.

"We're already out near the surf, then," Miguel said finally.

"Yeah. We swam fast."

"I've never seen so much fog."

"You very tired?" Rubén asked.

"Me? You crazy? Let's get going."

He immediately regretted saying that, but it was already too late. Rubén had said, "Okay, let's get going."

He succeeded in counting up to twenty strokes before telling himself he could not go on: he was hardly advancing; his right leg was half paralyzed by the cold, his arms felt clumsy and heavy. Panting, he yelled, "Rubén!" Rubén kept on swimming. "Rubén, Rubén!" He turned toward the beach and started to swim, to splash about, really, in desperation; and suddenly he was begging God to save him: he would be good in the future, he would obey his parents, he would not miss Sunday mass, and then he recalled having confessed to the Hawks that he only went to church "to see a chick" and he was sure as a knife stab that God was going to punish him by drowning him in those troubled waters he lashed so frantically, waters beneath which an atrocious death awaited him, and afterwards, perhaps, hell. Then, like an echo, there sprang to his mind a certain old saying sometimes uttered by Father Alberto in religion class, something about divine mercy knowing no bounds, and while he was flailing the sea with his arms— his legs hung like dead weights—with his lips moving, he begged God to be good to him, he was so young, and he swore he would go to the seminary if he was saved, but a second later, scared, he corrected himself, and promised that instead of becoming a priest he would make sacrifices and other things, he would give alms, and at that point he realized how hesitating and bargaining at such a critical moment could be fatal and then he heard Rubén's maddened shouts, very nearby, and he turned his head and saw him, about ten yards away, his face half sunk in the water, waving an arm, pleading: "Miguel, brother, come over here, I'm drowning, don't go away!"

He remained motionless, puzzled, and suddenly it was as though Rubén's desperation banished his own; he felt himself recovering his courage, felt the stiffness in his legs lessening.

"I've got a stomach cramp," Rubén shrieked. "I can't go any farther, Miguel. Save me, for God's sake. Don't leave me, brother."

He floated toward Rubén and was on the point of swimming up to him when he recalled that drowning people always manage to grab hold of their rescuers like pincers and take them down; and he swam off, but the cries terrified him and he sensed that if Rubén drowned, he would not be able to reach the beach either, and he turned back. Two yards from Rubén, who was quite white and shriveled, sinking and surfacing, he shouted: "Don't move, Rubén. I'm going to pull you but don't try to grab me; if you grab me we'll sink, Rubén. You're going to stay still, brother. I'm going to pull you by the head; don't touch me." He kept at a safe distance and stretched out a hand until he reached Rubén's hair. He began to swim with his free arm, trying with all his strength to assist with his legs. The movement was slow, very laborious. It sapped all his power and he was hardly aware of Rubén, complaining monotonously, suddenly letting out terrible screams— "I'm going to die, Miguel, save me"—or retching in spasms. He was exhausted when he stopped. With one hand he held Rubén up, with the other he traced circles on the surface. He breathed deeply through his mouth. Rubén's face was contracted in pain, his lips folded back in a strange grimace.

"Brother," murmured Miguel, "we've only got a little way to go. Try. Rubén, answer me. Yell. Don't stay like that."

He slapped him hard and Rubén opened his eyes; he moved his head weakly.

"Yell, brother," Miguel repeated. "Try to stretch. I'm going to rub your stomach. We've only got a little way to go; don't give up."

His hand searched under the water, found a hard knot that began at Rubén's navel and took up a large part of his belly. He went over it many times, first slowly, then hard, and Rubén shouted, "I don't want to die, Miguel, save me!"

He started swimming again, dragging Rubén by the chin this time. Whenever a wave overtook them, Rubén choked; Miguel yelled at him to spit. And he kept on swimming, without stopping for a moment, closing his eyes at times, excited because a kind of confidence had sprung up in his heart, a warm, proud, stimulating feeling that protected him against the cold and the fatigue. A rock grazed one of his legs and he screamed and hurried on. A moment later he was able to stand up and pass his arms around Rubén. Holding him pressed up against himself, feeling his head leaning on one of his shoulders, he rested for a long while. Then he helped Rubén to stretch out on his back and, supporting him with his forearm, forced him to stretch his knees; he massaged his stomach until the knot began to loosen. Rubén was not shouting anymore; he was doing everything to stretch out completely and was rubbing himself with both his hands.

"Are you better?"

"Yeah, brother, I'm okay now. Let's get out."

An inexpressible joy filled them as they made their way over rocks, heads bent against the undertow, not feeling the sea urchins. Soon they saw the sharp edges of the cliffs, the bathhouse, and finally, close to shore, the Hawks standing on the women's balcony, looking for them.

"Hey!" Rubén said.

"Yeah?"

"Don't say anything to them. Please don't tell them I called out. We've always been very close friends, Miguel. Don't do that to me."

"You really think I'm that kind of louse?" Miguel said. "Don't worry, I won't say anything."

They climbed out, shivering. They sat down on the steps in the midst of an uproar from the Hawks.

"We were about to send our sympathy to your families," Tobias said.

"You've been in for more than an hour," the Brain said. "C'mon, how did it turn out?"

Speaking calmly while he dried his body with his undershirt, Rubén explained: "Nothing to tell. We went out to the surf and came back. That's how we Hawks are. Miguel beat me. Just barely, by a hand. Of course, if it'd been in a swimming pool, he'd have made a fool of himself."

Slaps of congratulation rained down on Miguel, who had dressed without drying off.

"You're getting to be a man," Melanés told him.

Miguel did not answer. Smiling, he thought how that same night he would go to Salazar Park. All Miraflores would soon know, thanks to Melanés, that he had won the heroic contest and Flora would be waiting for him with glowing eyes. A golden future was opening before him.

The Challenge

We were drinking beer, like every Saturday, when Leonidas appeared in the doorway of the River Bar. We saw at once from his face that something had happened.

"What's up?" Leon asked.

Leonidas pulled up a chair and sat down next to us.

"I'm dying of thirst."

I filled a glass up to the brim for him and the head spilled over onto the table. Leonidas blew gently and sat pensively, watching how the bubbles burst. Then he drank it down to the last drop in one gulp.

"Justo's going to be fighting tonight," he said in a strange voice.

We kept silent for a moment. Leon drank; Briceño lit a cigarette.

"He asked me to let you know," Leonidas added. "He wants you to come."

Finally, Briceño asked: "How did it go?"

"They met this afternoon at Catacaos." Leonidas wiped his forehead and lashed the air with his hand; a few drops of sweat slipped from his fingers to the floor. "You can picture the rest."

"After all," Leon said, "if they had to fight, better that way, according to the rules. No reason to get scared either. Justo knows what he's doing."

"Yeah," Leonidas agreed, absent-mindedly. "Maybe it's better like that."

The bottles stood empty. A breeze was blowing and just a few minutes earlier, we had stopped listening to the neighborhood band from the garrison at Grau playing in the plaza. The bridge was covered with people coming back from the open-air concert and the couples who had sought out the shade of the embankment also began leaving their hiding places. A lot of people were going by the door of the River Bar. A few came in. Soon the sidewalk café was full of men and women talking loudly and laughing.

"It's almost nine," Leon said. "We better get going."

"Okay, boys," Leonidas said. "Thanks for the beer."

We left.

"It's going to be at 'the raft,' right?" Briceño asked.

"Yeah. At eleven. Justo'll look for you at ten-thirty, right here."

The old man waved good-bye and went off down Castilla Avenue. He lived on the outskirts of town, where the dunes started, in a lonely hut that looked as if it were standing guard over the city. We walked toward the plaza. It was nearly deserted. Next to the Tourist Hotel some young guys were arguing loudly. Passing by, we noticed a girl in the middle, listening, smiling. She was pretty and seemed to be enjoying herself.

"The Gimp's going to kill him," Briceño said suddenly.

"Shut up!" Leon snapped.

We went our separate ways at the corner by the church. I walked home quickly. Nobody was there. I put on overalls and two pullovers and hid my knife, wrapped in a handkerchief, in the back pocket of my pants. As I was leaving, I met my wife, just getting home.

"Going out again?" she asked.

"Yeah. I've got some business to take care of."

The boy was asleep in her arms and I had the impression he was dead.

"You've got to get up early," she insisted. "You work Sundays, remember?"

"Don't worry," I replied. "I'll be back in a few minutes."

I walked back down to the River Bar and sat at the bar. I asked for a beer and a sandwich, which I didn't finish. I'd lost my appetite. Somebody tapped me on the shoulder. It was Moses, the owner of the place.

"The fight's on?"

"Yeah. It's going to be at 'the raft.' Better keep quiet."

"I don't need advice from you," he said. "I heard about it a little while ago. I feel sorry for Justo, but really, he's been asking for it for some time. And the Gimp's not very patient—we all know that by now."

"The Gimp's an asshole."

"He used to be your friend . . ." Moses started to say, but checked himself.

Somebody was calling him from an outside table and he went off, but in a few minutes he was back at my side.

"Want me to go?" he asked.

"No. There's enough with us, thanks."

"Okay. Let me know if I can help some way. Justo's my friend too." He took a sip of my beer without asking. "Last night the Gimp was here with his bunch. All he did was talk about Justo and swear he was going to cut him up into little pieces. I was praying you guys wouldn't decide to come by here."

"I'd like to have seen the Gimp," I said. "His face is really funny when he's mad."

Moses laughed. "Last night he looked like the devil. And he's so ugly you can't look at him without feeling sick."

I finished my beer and left to walk along the embankment, but from the doorway of the River Bar I saw Justo, all alone, sitting at an outside table. He had on rubber sneakers and a faded pullover that came up to his ears. Seen from the side and against the darkness outside, he looked like a kid, a woman: from that angle, his features were delicate, soft. Hearing my footsteps, he turned around, showing me the purple scar wounding the other side of his face, from the corner of his mouth up to his forehead. (Some people say it was from a punch he took in a fight when he was a kid, but Leonidas insisted he'd been born the day of the flood and that scar was his mother's fright when she saw the water come right up to the door of the house.)

"I just got here," he said. "What's with the others?"

"They're coming. They must be on their way."

Justo looked at me straight on. He seemed about to smile, but got very serious and turned his head.

"What happened this afternoon?"

He shrugged and made a vague gesture.

"We met at the Sunken Cart. I just went in to have a drink and I bump into the Gimp and his guys face to face. Get it? If the priest hadn't stepped in, they'd have cut my throat right there. They jumped me like dogs. Like mad dogs. The priest pulled us apart."

"Are you a man?" the Gimp shouted.

"More than you," Justo shouted.

"Quiet, you animals," the priest said.

"At 'the raft' tonight, then?" the Gimp shouted.
"Okay," said Justo.
"That was all."

The crowd at the River Bar had dwindled. A few people were left at the bar but we were alone at an outside table.

"I brought this," I said, handing him the handkerchief. Justo opened the knife and hefted it. The blade was exactly the size of his hand, from his wrist to his fingernails. Then he took another knife out of his pocket and compared them.

"They're the same," he said. "I'll stick with mine."

He asked for a beer and we drank it without speaking, just smoking.

"I haven't got the time," said Justo, "but it must be past ten. Let's go catch up with them."

At the top of the bridge we met Briceño and Leon. They greeted Justo, shaking his hand.

"Listen, brother," Leon said, "you're going to cut him to shreds."

"That goes without saying," said Briceño. "The Gimp couldn't touch you."

They both had on the same clothes as before and seemed to have agreed on showing confidence and even a certain amount of lightheartedness in front of Justo.

"Let's go down this way," Leon said. "It's shorter."

"No," Justo said. "Let's go around. I don't feel like breaking my leg just now."

That fear was funny because we always went down to the riverbed by lowering ourselves from the steel framework holding up the bridge. We went a block farther on the street, then turned right and walked for a good while in silence. Going down the narrow path to the riverbed,

Briceño tripped and swore. The sand was lukewarm and our feet sank in as if we were walking on a sea of cotton. Leon looked attentively at the sky.

"Lots of clouds," he said. "The moon's not going to help much tonight."

"We'll light bonfires," Justo said.

"Are you crazy?" I said. "You want the police to come?"

"It can be arranged," Briceño said without conviction. "It could be put off till tomorrow. They're not going to fight in the dark."

Nobody answered and Briceño didn't persist.

"Here's 'the raft,' " Leon said.

At one time—nobody knew when—a carob tree had fallen into the riverbed and it was so huge that it stretched three quarters of the way across the dry riverbed. It was very heavy and once it went down, the water couldn't raise it, could only drag it along for a few yards, so that each year "the raft" moved a little farther from the city. Nobody knew, either, who had given it the name "the raft," but that's what everybody called it.

"They're here already," Leon said.

We stopped about five yards short of "the raft." In the dim glow of night we couldn't make out the faces of whoever was waiting for us, only their silhouettes. There were five of them. I counted, trying in vain to find the Gimp.

"You go," Justo said.

I moved toward the tree trunk slowly, trying to keep a calm expression on my face.

"Stop!" somebody shouted. "Who's there?"

"Julian," I called out. "Julian Huertas. You blind?"

A small shape came out to meet me. It was Chalupas.

"We were just leaving," he said. "We figured little Justo

had gone to the police to ask them to take care of him."

"I want to come to terms with a man," I shouted without answering him. "Not with this dwarf."

"Are you real brave?" Chalupas asked, with an edge in his voice.

"Silence!" the Gimp shouted. They had all drawn near and the Gimp advanced toward me. He was tall, much taller than all the others. In the dark I couldn't see but could only imagine the face armored in pimples, the skin, deep olive and beardless, the tiny pinholes of his eyes, sunken like two dots in that lump of flesh divided by the oblong bumps of his cheekbones, and his lips, thick as fingers, hanging from his chin, triangular like an iguana's. The Gimp's left foot was lame. People said he had a scar shaped like a cross on that foot, a souvenir from a pig that bit him while he was sleeping, but nobody had ever seen that scar.

"Why'd you bring Leonidas?" the Gimp asked hoarsely.

"Leonidas? Who's brought Leonidas?"

With his finger the Gimp pointed off to one side. The old man had been a few yards behind on the sand and when he heard his name mentioned he came near.

"What about me!" he said. He looked at the Gimp fixedly. "I don't need them to bring me along. I came along, on my own two feet, just because I felt like it. If you're looking for an excuse not to fight, say so."

The Gimp hesitated before answering. I thought he was going to insult the old man and I quickly moved my hand to my back pocket.

"Don't get involved, Pop," said the Gimp amiably. "I'm not going to fight with you."

"Don't think I'm so old," Leonidas said. "I've walked over a lot better than you."

"It's okay, Pop," the Gimp said. "I believe you." He turned to me. "Are you ready?"

"Yeah. Tell your friends not to butt in. If they do, so much the worse for them."

The Gimp laughed. "Julian, you know I don't need any backup. Especially today. Don't worry."

One of the men behind the Gimp laughed too. The Gimp handed something toward me. I reached out my hand: his knife blade was out and I had taken it by the cutting edge. I felt a small scratch in my palm and a trembling. The metal felt like a piece of ice.

"Got matches, Pop?"

Leonidas lit a match and held it between his fingers until the flame licked his fingernails. In the feeble light of the flame I thoroughly examined the knife. I measured its width and length; I checked the edge of its blade and its weight. "It's okay," I said.

"Chunga," the Gimp ordered. "Go with him."

Chunga walked between Leonidas and me. When we reached the others, Briceño was smoking and every drag he took lit up, for an instant, the faces of Justo, impassive, tight-lipped; Leon, chewing on something, maybe a blade of grass; and Briceño himself, sweating.

"Who told you you could come?" Justo asked harshly.

"Nobody told me," Leonidas asserted loudly. "I came because I wanted to. You want explanations from me?"

Justo didn't answer. I signaled to him and pointed out Chunga, who had kept a little ways back. Justo took out his knife and threw it. The weapon fell somewhere near Chunga's body and he shrank back.

"Sorry," I said, groping on the sand in search of the knife. "It got away from me. Here it is."

"You're not going to be so cute in a while," Chunga said.

Then, just as I had done, he passed his fingers over the blade by match light; he returned it to us without saying anything and went back to "the raft" in long strides. For a few minutes we were silent, inhaling the perfume from the cotton plants nearby, borne by a warm breeze in the direction of the bridge. On the two sides of the riverbed in back of us the twinkling lights of the city were visible. The silence was almost total; from time to time barking or braying ruptured it abruptly.

"Ready!" shouted a voice from the other side.

"Ready!" I shouted.

There was shuffling and whispering among the group of men next to "the raft." Then a limping shadow slid toward the center of the space the two groups had marked off. I saw the Gimp test the ground out there with his feet, checking whether there were stones, holes. My eyes sought out Justo: Leon and Briceño had put their arms on his shoulders. Justo detached himself from them quickly. When he was beside me, he smiled. I put out my hand to him. He started to back away but Leonidas jumped and grabbed him by the shoulders. The old man took off a poncho he was wearing over his back. He stood at my side.

"Don't get close to him even for a second." The old man spoke slowly, his voice trembling slightly. "Always at a distance. Dance round him till he's worn out. Most of all, guard your stomach and face. Keep your arm up all the time. Crouch down, feet firm on the ground. If you slip, kick in the air until he pulls back. . . . All right, get going. Carry yourself like a man. . . ."

Justo listened to Leonidas with his head lowered. I thought he was going to hug him but he confined himself to a brusque gesture. He yanked the poncho out of the old man's hands and wrapped it around his arm. Then he withdrew, walking on the sand with firm steps, his head up. As he walked away from us, the short piece of metal in his right hand shot back glints. Justo halted two yards away from the Gimp.

For a few seconds they stood motionless, silent, surely saying with their eyes how much they hated each other, observing each other, their muscles tight under their clothing, right hands angrily crushing their knives. From a distance, half hidden by the night's warm darkness, they didn't look so much like two men getting ready to fight as shadowy statues cast in some black material or the shadows of two young, solid carob trees on the riverbank, reflected in the air, not on the sand. As if answering some urgently commanding voice, they started moving almost simultaneously. Maybe Justo was first, a second earlier. Fixed to the spot, he began to sway slowly from his knees on up to his shoulders and the Gimp imitated him, also rocking without spreading his feet. Their postures were identical: right arm in front, slightly bent, with the elbow turned out, hands pointing directly at the adversary's middle, and the left arm, disproportionate, gigantic, wrapped in a poncho and crossed over like a shield at face height. At first only their bodies moved; their heads, feet and hands remained fixed. Imperceptibly, they both had been bending forward, arching their backs, flexing their legs as if to dive into the water. The Gimp was the first to attack: he jumped forward suddenly, his arm tracing a rapid circle. Grazing Justo without wounding him, the weapon had followed an incomplete path through the air when Justo, who was fast, spun around. Without dropping his guard, he wove a circle around the other man, sliding gently over the sand, at an ever increasing rate. The Gimp spun in place. He had bent lower, and as he turned himself round and round, following the direction of his rival, he trailed him constantly with his eyes, like a man hypnotized. Unexpectedly, Justo stood upright: we saw him fall on the other with his whole body and spring back to his spot in a second, like a jack-in-the-box.

"There," whispered Briceño. "He nicked him."

"On the shoulder," said Leonidas. "But barely."

Without having given a yell, still steady in his position, the Gimp went on dancing, while Justo no longer held himself to circling around him: he moved in and away from the Gimp at the same time, shaking the poncho, dropping and keeping up his guard, offering his body and whisking it away, slippery, agile, tempting and rejecting his opponent like a woman in heat. He wanted to get him dizzy, but the Gimp had experience as well as tricks. He broke out of the circle by retreating, still bent over, forcing Justo to pause and to chase after him, pursuing in very short steps, neck out, face protected by the poncho draped over his arm. The Gimp drew back, dragging his feet, crouching so low his knees nearly touched the sand. Justo jabbed his arm out twice and both times hit only thin air. "Don't get so close," Leonidas said next to me in a voice so low only I could hear him, just when that shape—the broad, deformed shadow that had shrunk by folding into itself like a caterpillar—brutally regained its normal height and, in growing as well as charging, cut Justo out of our view. We were breathless for one, two, maybe three seconds, watching the immense figure of the clinched fighters, and we heard a brief sound, the first we'd heard during the duel, similar to a belch. An instant later, to one side of the gigantic shadow another sprang up, this one thinner and more graceful, throwing up an invisible wall between the two fighters in two leaps. This time the Gimp began to revolve:

he moved his right foot and dragged his left. I strained my
eyes vainly to penetrate the darkness and read on Justo's
skin what had happened in those three seconds when the
adversaries, as close as two lovers, formed a single body.
"Get out of there!" Leonidas said very slowly. "Why the
hell you fighting so close?" Mysteriously, as if the light
breeze that was blowing had carried that secret message to
him, Justo also began to bounce up and down, like the
Gimp. Stalking, watchful, fierce, they went from defense to
attack and then back to defense with the speed of lightning,
but the feints fooled neither one: to the swift move of the
enemy's arm poised as if to throw a stone, which was in-
tended not to wound but to balk the adversary, to confuse
him for an instant, to throw him off guard, the other man
would respond automatically, raising his left arm without
budging. I wasn't able to see their faces, but I closed my
eyes and saw them better than if I'd been in their midst: the
Gimp sweating, his mouth shut, his little pig eyes aflame
and blazing behind his eyelids, his skin throbbing, the
wings of his flattened nose and the slit of his mouth shaken
by an inconceivable quivering; and Justo, with his usual
sneering mask intensified by anger and his lips moist with
rage and fatigue. I opened my eyes just in time to see Justo
pounce madly, blindly on the other man, giving him every
advantage, offering his face, foolishly exposing his body.
Anger and impatience lifted him off the ground, held him
oddly up in the air, outlined against the sky, smashed him
violently into his prey. The savage outburst must have surprised the Gimp, who briefly remained indecisive, and
when he bent down, lengthening his arm like an arrow,
hiding from our view the shining blade we followed in our
imagination, we knew that Justo's crazy action hadn't been
totally wasted. At the impact, the night enveloping us be-

came populated with deep, blood-curdling roars bursting
like sparks from the fighters. We didn't know then, we will
never know, how long they were clenched in that convul-
sive polyhedron; but even without distinguishing who was
who, without knowing whose arm delivered which blows,
whose throat offered up those roars that followed one another like echoes, we repeatedly saw the naked knife blades
in the air, quivering toward the heavens or in the midst of
the darkness, down at their sides, swift, blazing, in and out
of sight, hidden or brandished in the night as in some
magician's spectacular show.

We must have been gasping and eager, holding our
breath, our eyes popping, maybe whispering gibberish,
until the human pyramid cracked, suddenly cleaved
through its center by an invisible slash: the two were flung
back, as if magnetized from behind, at the same moment,
with the same violent force. They stayed a yard apart, panting. "We've got to stop them," said Leon's voice. "It's
enough." But before we tried to move, the Gimp had left
his position like a meteor. Justo didn't sidestep the lunge
and they both rolled on the ground. They twisted in the
sand, rolling over on top of each other, splitting the air with
slashes and silent gasps. This time the fight was over
quickly. Soon they were still, stretched out in the riverbed,
as if sleeping. I was ready to run toward them when, perhaps guessing my intention, someone suddenly stood up
and remained standing next to the fallen man, swaying
worse than a drunk. It was the Gimp.

In the struggle they had lost their ponchos, which lay a
little way off, looking like a many-faceted rock. "Let's go,"
Leon said. But this time as well something happened that
left us motionless. Justo got up with difficulty, leaning his
entire weight on his right arm and covering his head with

his free hand as if he wanted to drive some horrible sight away from his eyes. When he was up the Gimp stepped back a few feet. Justo swayed. He hadn't taken his arm from his face. Then we heard a voice we all knew but which we wouldn't have recognized if it had taken us by surprise in the dark.

"Julian!" the Gimp shouted. "Tell him to give up!"

I turned to look at Leonidas but I found his face blocked out by Leon's: he was watching the scene with a horrified expression. I turned back to look at them: they were joined once again. Roused by the Gimp's words, Justo, no doubt about it, had taken his arm from his face the second I looked away from the fight and he must have thrown himself on his enemy, draining the last strength out of his pain, out of the bitterness of his defeat. Jumping backward, the Gimp easily escaped this emotional and useless attack.

"Leonidas!" he shouted again in a furious, imploring tone. "Tell him to give up."

"Shut up and fight!" Leonidas bellowed without hesitating.

Justo had attempted another attack, but all of us, especially Leonidas, who was old and had seen many fights in his day, knew there was nothing to be done now, that his arm didn't have enough strength even to scratch the Gimp's olive-toned skin. With an anguish born in his depths and rising to his lips, making them dry, and even to his eyes, clouding them over, he struggled in slow motion as we watched for still another moment until the shadow crumpled once more: someone collapsed onto the ground with a dry sound.

When we reached the spot where Justo was lying, the Gimp had withdrawn to his men and they started leaving all together without speaking. I put my face next to his chest, hardly noticing that a hot substance dampened my neck and shoulder as my hand, through the rips in the cloth, explored his stomach and back, sometimes plunging into the limp, damp, cold body of a beached jellyfish. Briceño and Leon took off their jackets, wrapped him carefully and picked him up by his feet and arms. I looked for Leonidas's poncho, which lay a few feet away, and not looking, just groping, I covered his face. Then, in two rows, the four of us carried him on our shoulders like a coffin and we walked, matching our steps, in the direction of the path that climbed up the riverbank and back to the city.

"Don't cry, old-timer," Leon said. "I've never known anyone brave as your son. I really mean that."

Leonidas didn't answer. He walked behind me, so I couldn't see him.

At the first huts in Castilla, I asked: "Want us to carry him to your house, Leonidas?"

"Yes," the old man said hastily, as if he hadn't been listening.

The Younger Brother

There was an enormous rock at the side of the road and on the rock a toad. David took aim carefully.

"Don't shoot," Juan said.

Surprised, David lowered the weapon and looked at his brother.

"He can hear the shots," Juan said.

"Are you crazy? We're forty miles from the waterfall."

"Maybe he's not at the waterfall," Juan insisted, "but at the caves."

"No," David said. "Besides, even if he was, he'd never think it's us."

The toad sat there, breathing calmly, its gaping mouth wide open, while from behind its bleary eyes it was watching David with a certain sickly air. David raised the revolver, took aim slowly and fired.

"You didn't hit him," Juan said.

"Yes I did."

They went up to the rock. A small green blot marked the spot where the toad had been.

"Didn't I hit him?"

"Yes," Juan said, "you got him."

They walked toward the horses. The same stabbing, cold wind that had escorted them on their journey was blowing but the land was beginning to change: the sun sank behind the hills, a vague shadow cloaked the fields at the foot of a mountain, the clouds curled around the nearest peaks had taken on the dark gray color of the rocks. David threw around his shoulders the blanket he had spread on the ground in order to rest and then, mechanically, he replaced the used cartridge in his revolver. Out of the corner of his eye, Juan watched David's hands as he loaded the weapon and shoved it into its holster; his fingers seemed not to obey any intention but to act on their own.

"Want to move on?" David asked.

Juan agreed.

The road was a narrow slope and the animals climbed with difficulty, constantly slipping on the rocks, which were still wet from the past few days' rain. The brothers kept silent. A gentle and invisible drizzle greeted them a little after they started up again, but it stopped quickly. It was growing dark when they sighted the caves; the hill, which everyone called Hill of the Eyes, was blunted and stretched out like an earthworm.

"Want to see if he's there?" asked Juan.

"It's not worth the trouble. I'm sure he hasn't moved from the waterfall. He knows they could see him around here. Somebody's always going by on the road."

"Whatever you say," Juan said. And a minute later he asked, "What if that guy was lying?"

"Who?"

"The one who told us he saw him."

"Leandro? No, he wouldn't have the nerve to lie to me. He said he was hiding at the waterfall and it's a sure bet he's there. You'll see."

They continued onward until nightfall. A black sheet enveloped them and in the dark the desolation of that lonely region with neither trees nor people was visible only in the silence, which increased until it became an almost physical presence. Bent over the neck of his mount, Juan kept trying to make out the blurred traces of the path. He knew they had reached the peak when they unexpectedly found themselves on flat ground. David suggested that they continue on foot. They dismounted and tied the animals to some rocks. The older brother tugged at the mane of his horse, patted it on the flanks several times and whispered into its ear: "Hope we don't find you frozen tomorrow."

"Are we going down now?" Juan asked.

"Yes," David answered. "Aren't you cold? It's better to wait for daylight in the pass. We'll rest there. Scare you to go down in the dark?"

"No. Let's go down, if you want."

They began the descent immediately. David went first, carrying a small flashlight, and the column of light swung between his feet and Juan's, the golden circle pausing for a second on the spot where the younger brother should step. After a few minutes Juan was sweating heavily and the rough rocks on the hillside had covered his hands with scratches. All he could see was the illuminated disk in front of him, but he heard his brother's breathing and guessed at his movements: he must be advancing over the slippery decline very sure of himself, dodging the obstacles without difficulty. He, on the other hand, tested the solidity of the ground before each step and looked for some support to grab hold of. Even so, he was on the verge of falling several times. When they reached the chasm, Juan thought the descent had perhaps taken several hours. He was exhausted and now he could hear, very close by, the sound of the waterfall: a grand and majestic curtain of water falling from high up, resounding like thunder, into a lagoon feeding into a stream. Grass and moss grew around the lagoon all year long and that was the only vegetation for twenty miles around.

"Let's rest here," David said.

They sat down alongside each other. The night was cold, the air damp, the sky clouded over. Juan lit a cigarette. He was tired but not sleepy. He felt his brother stretch and yawn. A little later David stopped moving; his breathing was smoother and more rhythmical and from time to time he let out a sort of murmur. In turn, Juan tried to sleep. He made his body as comfortable as he could on the rocks and tried with no success to clear his brain. He lit another cigarette. When he had returned to the ranch three months ago, it had been two years since he had seen his brother and sister. David was the same person he had hated and admired ever since childhood, but Leonor had changed: she was no longer the little girl who used to poke her head in the windows of the shack in order to throw stones at the imprisoned Indians, but a tall woman with primitive gestures, and her beauty, like the countryside around her, had something brutal about it. An intense brilliance had appeared in her eyes. Juan felt a sickness that blurred his sight, an emptiness in his stomach as after a jab of anger every time he associated the image of the man they were hunting with the memory of his sister. Still, at dawn of that day when he saw Camilo cross the clearing separating the ranch house from the stables to get the horses ready, he had hesitated.

"Let's leave without making any noise," David had said. "It'll be better if she doesn't wake up."

Going down the steps of the ranch house on tiptoe and

along the abandoned road flanking the fields, he had a strange sensation of choking, as if he were on the highest peak in the mountains; he hardly felt the buzzing thicket of mosquitoes that hurled themselves at him viciously and bit every exposed portion of his city dweller's skin. When they began to climb the mountain the choking went away. He was not a good horseman and the precipice, spread out like a terrible temptation at the edge of the path which looked like a thin streamer, absorbed him. He was on guard all the time, watchful of his mount's every step and concentrating his willpower against the dizziness he felt would overcome him.

"Look!"

Juan trembled. "You scared me," he said. "I thought you were asleep."

"Be quiet! Look."

"What?"

"Over there. Look."

Level with the ground where the cascade's roar seemed to originate, there was a small, twinkling light.

"It's a campfire," David said. "I swear it's him. Let's go."

"Let's wait for it to get light," Juan whispered: suddenly his throat had gone dry and was burning. "If he starts running, we'll never catch up to him in this darkness."

"He can't hear us over the deafening roar of that water," David answered firmly, taking his brother by the arm. "Let's go."

Very slowly, his body bent as if for a leap, David began to slide forward, hugging the hill. Juan was at his side, stumbling, his eyes fixed on the light, which grew smaller and then larger as if someone were fanning the flame. The closer the brothers drew, the more the glare of the fire revealed the nearby ground: rough boulders, brambles, the edge of the lagoon, but no human figure. Nevertheless, Juan was certain now that the man they were stalking was there, sunk in those shadows, in a spot very close to the light.

"It's him," David said. "See?"

For a mere instant the fragile tongues of fire had lit up a dark and evasive profile seeking warmth.

"What're we going to do?" Juan whispered, halting. But David was no longer at his side; he was running toward the place where that fleeting face had emerged.

Juan closed his eyes and imagined the Indian: squatting, his hands stretched out toward the flames, his eyes irritated by the sputtering of the campfire. Suddenly something fell on him, and he had guessed it was some animal, when he felt two violent hands closing around his neck and he understood. He must have experienced infinite terror at this unexpected attack coming out of the darkness. Most likely he was not even trying to defend himself. At most, he contracted like a snail to make his body less vulnerable and opened his eyes wide, struggling to see his assailant in the dark. Then he recognized the voice: "What have you done, pig? What have you done, you worm?" Juan heard David and realized that David was kicking the man. Sometimes his kicks seemed to smash against the rocks on the bank, not against the Indian. That must have made him even angrier. At first, a low growl reached Juan's ears, as if the Indian were gargling, but afterwards he only heard David's enraged voice, his threats, his insults. Suddenly Juan found the revolver in his right hand, his finger pressing the trigger lightly. In astonishment he thought that if he shot he might also kill his brother, but he didn't put the weapon away and, on the contrary, he felt immensely calm as he approached the fire.

"Enough, David!" he shouted. "Shoot him. Don't hit him anymore."

There was no answer. Now Juan could not see them: interlocked, the Indian and his brother had rolled outside the ring lit by the campfire. He did not see them, but he heard the dry sound of the punches and, sometimes, a curse or a deep breath.

"David," Juan shouted, "get out of there. I'm going to shoot."

A captive of intense excitement, he repeated seconds later: "Let him go, David. I swear I'm going to shoot."

Still there was no answer.

After firing the first shot, Juan stood thunderstruck for a moment, but then, without aiming, he continued shooting, until he could hear the metallic vibration of the firing pin against the empty cartridge. He stood motionless; he did not feel the revolver come loose from his hands and fall to his feet. The noise of the waterfall had disappeared and a trembling ran through his whole body; his skin was bathed in sweat and he was scarcely breathing. Suddenly, he shouted: "David!"

"Here I am, you idiot," a frightened and angry voice answered at his side. "You realize you could've shot me too? Are you out of your mind?"

Juan spun on his heels, his hands extended, and he hugged his brother. Clinging to him, he stammered incomprehensible sounds; he groaned and did not seem to understand the words coming from David, who was trying to soothe him. For a long while, Juan kept repeating incoherent words, sobbing. When he became calm, he remembered the Indian: "And him, David?"

"Him?" David had recovered his poise and spoke firmly. "How do you think he is?"

The campfire continued to burn, but it was giving very little light. Juan grabbed the biggest firebrand and looked for the Indian. When he found him, he stood observing him for a moment with fascinated eyes and then the torch fell to the ground and went out.

"Did you see, David?"

"Yes, I saw. Let's get out of here."

Juan was rigid and deaf. As if dreaming, he felt that David was dragging him toward the hill. The climb took them a long time. With one hand David held the flashlight and with the other, Juan, who seemed like a rag: he slipped on even the firmest rocks and fell to the ground without reacting. At the summit, they collapsed, exhausted. Juan buried his head in his arms and lay stretched out, breathing in great gulps. When he sat up, he saw his brother examining him with the flashlight.

"You're wounded," David said. "I'm going to bandage you."

He tore his handkerchief in two and with each of the pieces he bandaged Juan's knees, which were showing through rips in his pants, bathed in blood.

"That's for now," David said. "We'll go back right away. They might get infected. You're not used to climbing mountains. Leonor will fix you up."

The horses were shivering and their muzzles were covered with blue foam. David wiped them off with his hand, stroked them on the flanks and rumps, tenderly clucked his tongue next to their ears. "Now we're going to get warm," he whispered to them.

It was growing light when they mounted. A feeble glow was encompassing the mountain region and a white lacquer spread along the broken horizon, but the chasms lay sunk in darkness. Before leaving, David took a long drink from his canteen and handed it to Juan, who did not want any. They rode all morning through a hostile countryside, letting the horses set their own pace. At noon they stopped and made coffee. David ate some of the cheese and the beans that Camilo had put in their saddlebags. At dusk they sighted two wooden sticks forming an X. From them hung a board on which could be read "The Aurora." The horses neighed: they recognized the sign marking the boundary line of the ranch.

"Good," David said. "It was about time. I'm bushed. How're those knees holding up?"

Juan did not answer.

"Any pain?" David insisted.

"Tomorrow I'm leaving for Lima," Juan said.

"What are you saying?"

"I'm not going back to the ranch. I'm fed up with the mountains. I'll always live in the city. I don't want anything to do with the country."

Juan looked straight ahead, avoiding David's probing eyes.

"You're upset now," David said. "It's natural. We'll talk later."

"No," Juan said. "Let's talk now."

"Okay," David said gently. "What's the matter with you?"

Juan turned toward his brother; his face was washed out, his voice rasping. "What's wrong with me? Do you realize what you're saying? Have you forgotten that guy at the waterfall? If I stay at the ranch I'm going to end up thinking it's normal to do things like that."

He was going to add, "like you," but he did not dare.

"He was a sick dog," David said. "Your scruples are foolish. Maybe you've forgotten what he did to your sister?"

At that moment Juan's horse balked and started bucking and rearing on his back legs.

"He's going to bolt, David!" Juan said.

"Let go of his reins. You're choking him."

Juan loosened the reins and the animal calmed down.

"You haven't answered me," David said. "Have you forgotten why we went looking for him?"

"No," Juan answered. "I haven't forgotten."

Two hours later they reached Camilo's cabin, built on a promontory between the ranch house and the stables. Before the brothers drew to a halt, the cabin door opened and Camilo appeared in the doorway. Straw hat in hand, head lowered with respect, he came toward them and stopped between the two horses, whose reins he clasped.

"Everything all right?" David asked.

Camilo shook his head no. "Miss Leonor . . ."

"What's happened to Leonor?" Juan interrupted, standing up in the stirrups.

In his slow, muddled speech, Camilo explained that from her bedroom window Miss Leonor had seen the brothers leave at dawn and that when they were only about a thousand yards from the house, she had appeared on the grounds in boots and riding outfit, shouting orders for her horse to be saddled. Following David's instructions, Camilo refused to obey her. Then, by herself, she entered the stables resolutely and, like a man, with her own hands, placed the saddle, blankets and equipment on the roan, the ranch's smallest and most nervous horse, which was also her favorite.

When she was ready to mount, the servants from the house and Camilo himself had held her back; for a long while they endured insults and slaps from the exasperated girl, who argued and begged and demanded that they let her follow after her brothers.

"But," David stopped him, "did she know we . . . ?"

Always going slowly, taking care to choose his words and give them a humble and respectful turn, Camilo replied that yes, the girl knew where her brothers had gone.

"Oh, she'll pay for that!" David said. "It's Jacinta, I'm sure of it. She heard us talking that night with Leandro when she was serving dinner. It was her."

The girl had been very much affected, Camilo went on. After insulting and scratching the maids and himself, she began crying loudly and went back to the house. She had remained there ever since, shut up in her room.

The brothers left their horses with Camilo and headed for the house.

"Leonor mustn't know one word about this," Juan said.

"Of course not," David said. "Not one word."

Leonor knew they had gotten back by the dogs' barking. She was half asleep when a hoarse growl broke the night and under her window a panting animal passed by like a streak of lightning. It was Spooky. She recognized his frantic pacing and his unmistakable howling. Immediately, she heard the lazy trot and dull yowl of Domitila, the pregnant bitch. The dogs' aggressiveness stopped abruptly; the barking gave way to the eager panting with which they always greeted David. Through a slit in the blinds she saw her brothers approaching the house and heard the sound of the front door opening and closing. She waited for them to come upstairs and reach her room. When she opened the door, Juan was stretching out his hand to knock.

"Hello, little Leonor," David said.

She let them hug her and she brushed their foreheads with her lips, but she did not kiss them. Juan lit the lamp.

"Why didn't you let me know? You should have told me. I wanted to overtake you but Camilo wouldn't let me. You have to punish him, David. If you'd seen how he grabbed me. He's disobedient and rude. I kept begging him to let me go and he wouldn't pay any attention to me."

She had started speaking forcefully, but her voice broke. Her hair was uncombed and she was barefoot. David and Juan tried to calm her by stroking her hair, smiling at her, calling her baby sister.

"We didn't want to upset you," David explained. "Besides, we decided to go at the last minute. You were still asleep."

"What happened?" Leonor asked.

Juan took a blanket off the bed and put it around his sister. Leonor had stopped crying. She was pale; her mouth was half open and her gaze was filled with anxiety.

"Nothing," David said. "Nothing happened. We didn't find him."

The tension vanished from Leonor's face and an expression of relief came to her lips.

"But we will find him," David said. With a vague gesture he indicated to Leonor that she should go to bed. Then he turned around.

"Just a second; don't go," Leonor said.

Juan had not moved.

"Yes?" David said. "What's the matter, Leonor?"

"Don't go looking for him anymore."

"Don't you worry," David said. "Forget about all that. It's a matter for men. Leave it to us."

Then Leonor started crying again, this time with wild gestures. She raised her hands to her head, her whole body seemed electrified and her wailing alarmed the dogs, who began barking under her window. With a gesture, David signaled to Juan to do something, but the younger brother stood silent and motionless.

"All right, Leonor," David said. "Don't cry. We won't go looking for him."

"That's a lie. You're going to kill him. I know you."

"No I won't," David said. "If you think that skunk doesn't deserve to be punished . . ."

"He didn't do a thing to me," Leonor said very quickly, biting her lips.

"Don't think about it anymore," David insisted. "We'll forget all about him. Calm down, Leonor."

Leonor went on crying; her cheeks and lips were moist and the blanket had fallen to the floor.

"He didn't do anything to me," she repeated. "It was a lie."

"Do you know what you're saying?" David asked.

"I couldn't stand his following me everywhere," Leonor stammered. "He was after me all day long, like a shadow."

"It's my fault," David said bitterly. "It's dangerous for a woman to walk around the countryside by herself. I ordered him to protect you. I shouldn't have trusted an Indian. They're all alike."

"He didn't do anything to me, David," Leonor cried. "Believe me, I'm telling you the truth. Ask Camilo; he knows nothing happened. That's why he helped him get away. Didn't you know that? Yes, it was him. I told him to. I only wanted to get free of him, that's why I invented that story. Camilo knows everything; ask him."

Leonor dried her cheeks with the back of her hand. She picked up the blanket and threw it over her shoulders. She seemed to have shaken off a nightmare.

"We'll talk about this tomorrow," David said. "We're tired now. We've got to sleep."

"No," Juan said.

Leonor became aware how close her brother was: she had forgotten that Juan was there too. His forehead was full of wrinkles; the wings of his nose were throbbing, like Spooky's snout.

"You're going to repeat what you just said," Juan said to her in a strange way. "You're going to repeat how you lied to us."

"Juan," David said. "I hope you're not going to believe her. She's trying to trick us now."

"I've told the truth," Leonor roared. She was looking from one brother to the other. "I ordered him to leave me alone that day and he wouldn't. I went to the river and there he was, behind me. I couldn't even go swimming in peace. He'd stand there, sizing me up on the sly, like an animal. Then I came and told you that."

"Juan, wait," David said. "Where're you going? Wait!"

Juan had turned around and was heading toward the door; when David tried to stop him, he exploded. Like someone possessed, he began shouting insults: he called his sister a whore and his brother a swine and a tyrant. Violently he pushed David, who tried in vain to block his way, and he left the house in great strides, trailing a stream of insults. From the window, Leonor and David saw him cross the grounds at a full run, shouting like a madman, and they saw him go into the stables and come out, riding the roan bareback. At first, Leonor's temperamental horse tamely followed the direction indicated by the inexperienced fists holding the reins: turning with elegance, changing step and waving the light hair of its tail like a fan, the roan got as far as the edge of the road that led through mountains, through narrow passes and vast sandy expanses, to the city. There it rebelled. Suddenly rearing up and neighing, it spun like a ballerina and swiftly returned to the ground.

"It's going to throw him," Leonor said.

"No," said David at her side. "Look. He's holding on."

Many Indians had come out of the stable and in amazement were watching the younger brother, who held himself unbelievably steady on the horse and at the same time ferociously kicked its flanks and pounded its head with one of his fists. Enraged by the blows, the roan went from one side to the other, rearing, jumping; it started dizzying, abrupt runs and suddenly stopped dead, but the rider seemed soldered to its back. Leonor and David saw him appear and disappear as steady as the most seasoned horse tamer, and they were mute, stunned. Suddenly the roan gave up; its graceful head hanging down toward the ground as if ashamed, it stood motionless, breathing heavily. At that moment they thought he was coming back: Juan headed the horse toward the house and stopped in front of the door, but he did not dismount. As if he had remembered something, he turned around and headed at a fast trot directly toward the building called the Shack. There he jumped down. The door was locked and Juan kicked the padlock off. Then he shouted at the Indians who were inside to get out, that the punishment for all of them was over. After that, he came back to the house, walking slowly. David was waiting for him at the door. Juan seemed calm; he was drenched in sweat and his eyes showed his pride. David came up to him and brought him inside, his arm around Juan's shoulder.

"C'mon," he said to him. "We'll have a drink while Leonor fixes up your knees."